Twin Flame Trilogy

CINDY M. RANKIN

crippledbeaglepublishing.com
Knoxville, Tennessee

Cover design by Jody Dyer and Cindy M. Rankin

Paperback ISBN 978-1-958533-08-6
Hardcover ISBN 978-1-958533-09-3

Library of Congress Control Number: 2022918079

Printed in the United States of America

To my husband, Wayne, thank you for all your patience, love, understanding, and letting me free to finish this journey.

To my sister, Tina, thank you for listening and advising me all hours of the day. You have always been my rock.

To two sisters, Cindy and Cece, for letting me take a booth at their restaurant and create most of my story.

To the sheriff who gave me a spark and made me feel I knew him when we never met in this lifetime. See you in the next.

To the many angels, who helped with details in my story to make it right.

To Jody, for making this story real.

To Bess, for being the only brave person to read my story to see if it was worthy to publish and give me great feedback.

Thank you. God bless.

Twin Flame Trilogy

Part I: The Beginning 9

Chapter 1: 1,000 B.C. 11

Chapter 2: Newborns, 500 B.C. 16

Chapter 3: The Meeting 22

Chapter 4: Two Days Later 24

Chapter 5: Two Weeks Later 27

Part II: We Meet Again 33

Chapter 1: Mid-September 1876 35

Chapter 2: The Birthday Dinner 48

Chapter 3: The Church Picnic 54

Chapter 4: Cemetery and Mitchell 66

Chapter 5: Fishing and Mitchell 70

Chapter 6: Engagement and Wedding 80

Chapter 7: Honeymoon 87

Chapter 8: Vadoma and the Dark Figure 96

Part III: Never-Ending Love 100

Chapter 1: February 11, 2021 102

Chapter 2: The First Meeting 109

Chapter 3: I Know You're There 113

Chapter 4: The Foretelling Gift 115

Chapter 5: Second Meeting 121

Chapter 6: First Date 126

Chapter 7: Father and Son Talk and Sister to Sister Talk 136

Chapter 8: Second Date – The Barbecue 141

Chapter 9: Meeting the Family 146

Chapter 10: Jackie's Dinner Party 155

Chapter 11: Mary's Birthday Luncheon 161

Chapter 12: Halloween and the Musketeer Girls 163

Chapter 13: The Special Date 169

Chapter 14: The Promise 180

About the Author 181

Twin Flame

By Cindy M. Rankin

One's soul burns bright as a flame
Sometimes it will split into two
Both exactly identical, female and male.
Each on a soul's journey to grow
Teaching each other every time they meet
To heal, learn, create, forgive, and love
To help each reach the next level
Of enlightenment and to burn bright
Again and again, for all eternity
This is a twin flame!

Part I: The Beginning

Chapter 1: 1,000 B.C.

The large, clustered cloud was not pure white. It had an opalescent luster, which gave it an angelic look. The atmosphere sparkled with electricity and power.

A limestone pedestal rested in the center of the cloud. Upon it, Zeus sat engulfing the plain, smooth, golden throne. With his over-empowering persona, the throne needn't be ornate. Though simplistic in design, the brilliance radiated the power of its occupant.

A row of high-back marble chairs was arranged at floor level. There sat Zeus's court at his feet. Mighty in their own power but obedient to the divine.

Young Poseidon knelt before them and patiently waited for Zeus's next command.

"Poseidon, you have done me well for so long. It is my command for you to go and claim a place of your own to call home. This is your reward. I will always be watching you. Now, go with my blessing, and go in peace," Zeus's voice commanded. Zeus gave Poseidon a smile and then watched him stand and reverently back out of the cloud.

Poseidon had traveled far and wide. The heavens were full of wonderful places, but the weather, the people, and the lack of large bodies of water just didn't speak to him. He was trying a new place called Earth. It had many large bodies of water and many different types of land.

He discovered a sea with colors he had never seen before: turquoise, soft, deep blues and greens. The sea shimmered like bright, white stars. The sea was called the Caribbean. His heart raced, and his mind was in awe. There amongst the sea were several lands to explore. The largest one to the north attracted his attention. The sandy coast went into lush greens, then large hills in the center. He was fascinated by the many rings of waterways circling throughout the island. A large canal stretched from the Caribbean Sea to the foot of the southern part of the hills. It showed innovation for transportation. The people would be intelligent.

This could be the place, Poseidon thought. Ships floated through the canal and rings of water. Fishing and transporting goods made these waterways valuable. He visited several villages along his journey. They were friendly and hard workers. He would make this island his home and call it "Atlantis."

On Atlantis, the next village he came to was having a festival of some sort. Tables were laden with food, water, wine, greenery, and flowers. Music filled the air. A man of simple brown clothing, graying brown hair, and dark brown eyes came up to Poseidon.

"Welcome." He bowed. "We are thanking the gods for a wonderful and fruitful year. You are more than welcome here. Please join us. I am Leo."

Poseidon bowed. "I am called Poseidon."

Leo recognized the famous man before him. He bowed again. "It's an honor to welcome you here. Please join us. Follow me to my family's table."

At a long table sat a lovely lady, who was short with long, graying blonde hair that lay plaited down her back.

"Diona, may I present our guest, Poseidon," Leo said proudly.

With a surprised and warming smile, Diona gently replied, "It is an honor to have you as our guest."

Her turquoise eyes sparkled, and Poseidon was intrigued by the color. Never before had he seen such beautiful eyes. Diona turned to a young lady's back. Her long, blonde, plaited hair was fashioned with tiny, colorful flowers. Diona tapped her daughter's shoulder to get her attention.

"Clieto, you must meet our honored guest."

Clieto turned. The same striking turquoise eyes stared into Poseidon's deep, ocean blue eyes. Sparks were felt between them. Desire ran through their bodies. Everyone felt the chemistry between them.

Diona interrupted the intense moment. "Clieto, this is Poseidon. Poseidon, this is our daughter, Clieto."

He wanted to speak the words in his mind, but he couldn't. She took his breath and voice.

Leo was no fool and would be thrilled to have Poseidon as a son-in-law. So, he placed Poseidon between his wife and daughter. Diona moved over on the long bench for Poseidon and Leo to sit down.

After the shock, Poseidon finally composed himself. He turned to Clieto. "It's a pleasure to meet such a beautiful lady."

Clieto blushed bright red.

"Thank you. Never have I met such a striking man," Clieto replied.

"Thank you," replied Poseidon.

They ate their meal in silence, neither looking at the other out of awkward fear of the powerful connection happening between them.

—

The days that followed, Poseidon took rule over Atlantis. With thoughts of Clieto, he built a fortress on top of the hill in the middle of Atlantis and called it "Hill Clieto" after his love. There, he married her, had children, and ruled thoughtfully, gracefully, and righteously in honor of Zeus. Life was good.

Chapter 2: Newborns, 500 B.C.

Atlantis was now ruled by Poseidon's eldest son, Atlas, and his wife, Pleione, with their children. Atlas followed character in ruling Atlantis, but his brothers and other Titans were growing restless and upset with Zeus. Atlas kept the peace but wondered how long it would last.'

In the south between Hill Clieto and the Caribbean Sea, just a mile west of the canal, sat a three-story priestess temple at the edge of a thick forest. The limestone structure had two large, wooden entrance doors, and tall, open windows that were embraced by wooden shutters on each side for weather and to protect against intruders.

The first floor contained an expansive entrance with several wooden visitor benches. There was the high priestess's simple office, a kitchen, a large meal room, a library, and a temple for their ceremonies and prayers.

The second floor was arranged into three large rooms: one for healing people, a work and storage room for alchemists, and last, a birthing room.

The third floor held a sewing room, a large wardrobe closet, and several bedrooms. High

Priestess Artemis had her own room with a small balcony. How she enjoyed her perch! What views! How tranquil. What visions she had seen from that vantagepoint.

The tall, slender, dark-haired, and blue-eyed High Priestess Artemis looked out the second-floor birthing room's open window. The cool night breeze caressed her cheeks. Her long black robe comforted her like loving arms and gave her reassurance about what she needed to do next.

The bright navy sky was aflutter with meteor showers, dancing to the music of the universe. The brilliant white moon was fading as Venus moved across his face, and all would be soon blackened out. The event wouldn't matter to the stars; they would keep on dancing for the universe.

Darkness filled the room, and even the candles did little to show the scene that was taking place. All was still. The suspense was building.

A picture became crystal clear to her. A soul shining bright like a candle flame shone before her. In a blink of an eye, it split into alpha and omega, two exact flames of embodiment, two eternal twin flames. They would forever come together, love, learn, grow on their journey, die, and repeat the pattern for all eternity. She closed her eyes. The prophecy had been envisioned.

Little by little, the room filled once again with the loving moon's brightness.

All will be well, thought Artemis.

A loud scream brought Artemis back into the room's activity. Two women were ready to give life tonight. What a blessed night it would be!

Artemis turned around and went to the stand with cleansing lotion, a bowl of water, and a towel. She lathered her hands, then rinsed them in the cool water. Rubbing her hands dry, she approached the woman, Hebe, as Hebe let out another scream. Another priestess was dabbing cool water to Hebe's face.

"It will be any time now. Let me see what's going on," said Artemis. She placed the towel back on the stand, then went to the foot of the bed. Gently, she folded back the blanket to Hebe's waist. There between Hebe's legs, dark hair was crowning. It was always such a surprise and joy to see this happen.

Cupping her hands to either assist or catch, depending on the baby, Artemis demanded, "Push down hard, as hard as you can. The baby is coming."

Now, shoulders and chest had appeared.

"This time, push with all your soul and might!"

Hebe grunted as she pushed down as hard as she could. Suddenly, there was a squishing sound, then the cry of a baby.

"A perfect boy! He is quite handsome, with dark hair and blue eyes! What will you call him?" asked Artemis.

"Ares," replied Hebe.

Artemis took care of the baby's cord, then handed Ares to the other priestess to clean him up before presenting him to his mother.

"Let's get you ready for Ares, Hebe. We must take care of the afterbirth and clean you. Then you can feed your son." Artemis busied herself with her tasks. Just as she was almost finished, the other woman, Rhea, screamed.

Artemis rubbed more cleansing lotion and rinsed and her hands. Rhea screamed again. Another priestess was cooling Rhea's face. Artemis approached the foot of the bed and gently folded back the blanket. There between Rhea's legs, a blonde head of hair was crowning.

"It is your turn, Rhea! Push down hard. Someone is ready to come out," exclaimed Artemis. Rhea pushed down as hard as she could with a grunt. Shoulders and chest appeared. "One more big push!"

Rhea did her best, and out popped a crying baby.

"She is absolutely the most beautiful baby girl I've ever seen! What will you call her?"

"Pisces," replied Rhea.

Artemis finished with Pisces, then handed her to the priestess to clean before presenting her to Rhea. Artemis retrieved the afterbirth and bathed Rhea. Once done, both mothers were nursing with pride and joy. Artemis stood between the beds and admired the joyous event.

"This is a special night. I foresee these two souls to be special. They will love each other for all time. Keep them separate until they are fifteen years of age. This is because their love will be so strong that they will not know how to handle it. At that time, you both will hold a feast to announce their engagement and for them to first meet. You will hold their wedding within three months' time as is the custom. I warn you, let no one interfere! The heavens have blessed this union."

Artemis took from her pocket a bottle of special oil. With her fingertips of her right hand, she dabbed the oil to each of the babies' foreheads as she quietly said a blessing. Quietly, she left.

Artemis ascended the stairs to her room. She hoped she would live long enough to see them married. She undressed and put on her nightgown. Drawn to her balcony, she went out to view the ending of the show. The sun would soon lighten the skies, and all would begin. *Life can be so short but begin again and again*, she thought. She would have dreams about the children as she always did. Sometimes the dreams were wonderful, and sometimes they were a curse. She went to her bed, got under the covers, and dreamt.

Chapter 3: The Meeting
15 Years Later

Both villages were busy with preparations for the betrothal feast. Women were preparing savory and sweet dishes. Men were roasting meats and fish and making tables and benches. Elder women and young girls picked greenery and flowers. Older men and young boys brewed various wines. All would be put together at Pisces's village in two days' time.

Rhea watched her daughter helping her aunts stuff figs with almonds. This treat was Pisces's favorite. *What a lovely and sweet young woman Pisces has grown into*, thought Rhea. Pisces came up to her daydreaming mother and asked, "Mother, do you think he will love me?"

Rhea lovingly stroked Pisces's right cheek. "Yes, my love. Artemis saw in the stars the night you both were born. I've been told he is handsome, kind, and strong. Those are good qualities in a husband."

"Where will we live?" asked Pisces.

"I don't know. The fathers will discuss all in two weeks at Ares's house. Don't worry. No one in Atlantis lives that far away. We'll visit often. All will be well. Just open your heart to him, and you will be happy." Those were the words of wisdom Rhea's mother had told her the night before she wed.

Several women sat in another room and worked on Pisces's dress of turquoise, while others embroidered tiny flowers and greenery on a white dress for her wedding. Such tedious work was done with much love and many well wishes.

In Ares's village, the people were busy just like in Pisces's. Ares was helping his father keep the fires going under the roasting meats. He stepped in front of his father, Pericles, and asked, "Da, what if I don't like her?"

His father laughed wholeheartedly. "I heard she is the most beautiful woman Artemis has ever seen. Her people adore and praise her. She is kind, selfless, and upstanding." Pericles took a deep breath and sighed, "Besides, it was foretold that you will have a forever love with Pisces. Can't beat that. Don't worry. Just open your heart up to her, and you will have great happiness, as Da told me. It works!" He hugged Ares, then handed him more wood for the fire.

Chapter 4: Two Days Later

People woke up early to get everything set up for the celebration. Everyone from both villages worked together. The tables were adorned with plates, glasses, and floral arrangements. Musicians were warming up, which made setting everything up more enjoyable. Other tables were laden with food, water, and wine. The young would be serving. No idle hands here. It was just past midday when all was ready for a perfect day.

Atlas needed to attend a meeting with angry Titans, but he would be back for the wedding. Ares and his parents, Hebe and Pericles, wore royal blue and white with gold trim. Pisces and her parents, Rhea and Leo, were dressed in turquoise and white with silver trim.

Ares's family started at one end, walking to the center of the main table with Ares three feet behind. Pisces's family started from the opposite end with Pisces also three feet behind.

Neither Ares nor Pisces could see each other until Ares's father introduced them. Once the parents met at the center of the table, they bowed respectfully in greeting. The mothers moved aside. The fathers introduced their children.

Ares and Pisces looked deep into each other's eyes. Sparks flew between them. They both lost their breath as electricity ran through their bodies. They both thought the same thought: *How could anyone feel such intensity about someone the moment of just one, first look?*

Pericles broke the silence. "Ares, may I present Pisces. Pisces, may I present my son, Ares." He then placed the children's right hands together and announced loudly so all could hear, "I proclaim Ares to wed Pisces in three months' time. Gods bless this union."

Ares took his left hand and pulled out of his pocket a ring with a large, oval turquoise surrounded by smaller, round turquoise set in a gold filigree band. He had been told of Pisces' beautiful turquoise eyes and thought this ring would be perfect. The ring fit perfectly. Pisces was stunned by its beauty and workmanship. Ares said softly, "I betroth thee."

Everyone yelled with excitement. All but Leo sat down. Leo gave a blessing of thanks, then raised his glass of wine. Everyone raised their glasses. Leo yelled out, "Bless this couple. May their love shine and grow forever."

The people roared. Then all drank to toast the couple.

Ares and Pisces ate very little. They were too excited. They didn't dare look at each other until it was time to say goodbye.

Ares said, "I cannot wait to see you again in two weeks when you and your parents come to our home. I hope I have not been a disappointment to you."

Pisces softly responded, "You have not disappointed me. I hope I haven't disappointed you."

Ares felt such a strange need to protect her. Then, he answered, "You are the most beautiful woman I have ever met. I cannot wait to get to know you better when we next meet."

"I also cannot wait. I love my ring. Thank you. Until we meet again," she replied.

They would have such wonderful dreams until their next meeting. The strong feelings were beyond their expectations.

Chapter 5: Two Weeks Later

Everyone was eating breakfast when a messenger arrived to deliver a gift from Ares for Pisces. Pisces, curious, opened the engraved wooden box and found a pair of matching oval turquoise drop earrings. Her eyes became teary.

"They are beautiful! Please thank Ares for me. Tell him I shall wear them today with love," she said.

The messenger bowed and departed to deliver the loving message. Ares was delighted with her response. It gave him the hope that their marriage would be wonderful. He couldn't wait to see her again. What he wanted to do with her … that would have to wait.

Ares and his parents awaited Pisces and her family's arrival in the front courtyard. They were dressed in the same fashion they donned at the engagement feast. They heard the horses coming and called for the groomsmen to be ready to take the horses. As Leo and Rhea approached, a groomsman helped Rhea down, then took both horses away.

Ares came quickly to Pisces's side and helped her down. Their contact sent chills through both their bodies. Her horse was quickly taken away by another groomsman. Pisces was dressed in white, with butterflies and dragonflies embroidered into the fabric. Her blonde hair was once again plaited along her back. She took Ares' outstretched arm. Once again, chills ran through them.

"I am honored to see you again," whispered Ares.

Pisces's face flushed. She said, "And I, you."

The young couple was again seated side by side at the center of the table. Mothers were placed on one side and the fathers on the other side. The mothers planned the wedding feast, and the fathers discussed living quarters and other related matters. Ares and Pisces discussed their likes and dislikes and found that they were not only attracted to each other, but they also had a lot in common.

"The earrings match your eyes perfectly," said Ares.

"They are beautiful. Thank you so much for them," replied Pisces.

"Not as beautiful as your eyes," Ares said, smirking, and Pisces laughed.

The meal was delicious, but again, the young couple ate little. Suddenly, the sky darkened, and the ground began to tremble. Items not removed from the table fell to the floor, as did the people who were not seated. Animals started to cry. The ground shook harder. Everyone, even the seated, fell to the floor. The men covered the women with their bodies for protection. Ares covered Pisces. He didn't want to lose her after just meeting her. They had a lifetime, didn't they?

Zeus roared as loudly as all the heavens, and Earth heard. He was enraged at the betrayal of the Titans. How could they want to kill him? The Titans and their families were going to pay. Thunder and large bolts of lightning began striking with intensity. This time, the ground shook more violently, causing the ground beneath them to crack. The cracks became larger, making the surrounding land and all who inhabited it fall into the crevices.

A loud, whooshing sound startled everyone. Children and women wailed in fear. The sound grew louder. The Caribbean Sea built a high wall of a wave that came racing with fury toward Atlantis. As quick as a blink of an eye, all of Atlantis was engulfed by the Caribbean Sea. Another roar sounded from Zeus, followed by more thunder and lightning bolts. Zeus's wrath against the Titans and their loved ones was felt throughout the heavens.

Then, all was quiet.

There was nothing left of Atlantis—no debris, no land, no people, no trace. The scene appeared as if Atlantis had never existed. Atlantis was buried at the bottom of the sea.

"A lesson to you all!" cried Zeus.

All was engulfed by the sea. Atlantis and all its inhabitants were gone forever, except for Atlas.

—

The next day, the sky was bright and clear. The sea waters were calm and sparkled like stars. Sea birds freely flew, and the fish swam happily as if nothing had happened.

"This area will always be the sea. No land or people will ever live here. I will call this area the Bermuda Triangle," exclaimed Zeus.

Atlas knelt before Zeus. He awaited his sentence.

"I have never been so angry! I have incarcerated all the Titans in Tartarus for fighting against me. As for you, Atlas," Zeus paused in thought, "I know you tried to keep peace, but you too went against me. For that, your punishment is to have the burden of shouldering the heavens for all eternity."

Meekly, Atlas raised his eyes to meet Zeus's and inquired, "What about Ares and Pisces?"

"I have not forgotten about them. One day, I might allow them to come back together," Zeus replied. A large grin grew upon Zeus's face, and he laughed, then added, "Or maybe not."

Part II: We Meet Again

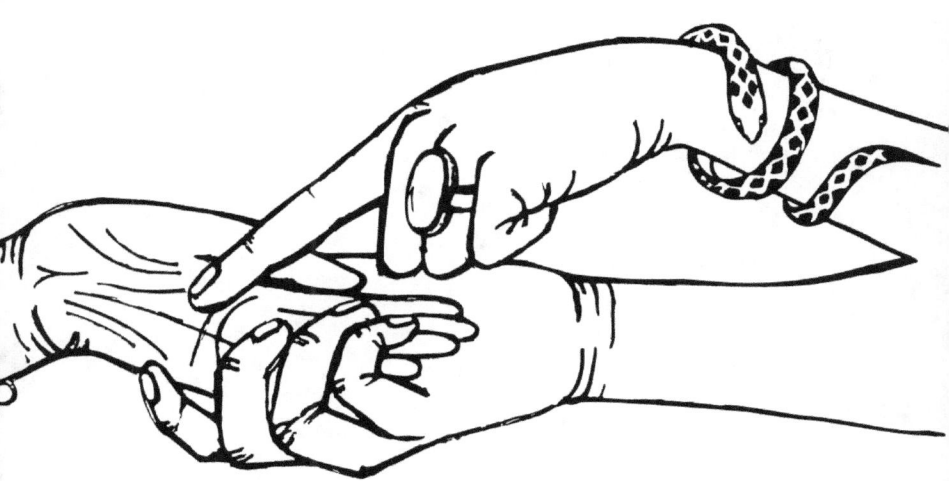

Chapter 1: Mid-September 1876

Charlottesville, Virginia was like a Sleepy Hollow during the Civil War. To its north, Rio Hill was the closest disaster; otherwise, the battles raged sixty miles to the north, south, east, and west. Though Confederate until near the end, most of Charlottesville's population grew due to the incoming of slaves, freed slaves, indentured foreigners, displaced families, and a few gypsies. Jobs grew during and after the war. Newspapers, uniforms, clothing, food, ammunition, horses, grain mills, lumber mills, field hands, domestic help, hospital help, restaurant help, and store help were all much in demand.

Most plantation owners were fair masters, so life on these estates ran pretty much the same after the war, but everyone still minded their p's and q's. The University of Virginia's enrollment dropped to only forty-six students as the rest went off to soldier in the war. Most of the university housed injured soldiers. The university hospital was famous for its artificial limbs, which surpassed the quality of the French limbs.

South of the city rested several plantations and Michie Tavern and Inn. The lifestyle there never lost its "southern charm." The largest plantation was Monticello; its 5,000 acres were impressive. Near the main house was Mulberry Road, which housed servants in one or two-bedroom cabins. This was luxury for them at this time.

Michie Tavern and Inn was east of Monticello. It was a coaching stop, restaurant, inn, center of life for the city and country folk, a place for doctors and dentists to see patients, and a place for a man to have a drink and discuss local affairs or anything else which men liked to discuss.

West of Monticello rested Tifton. In the northern part, there sat Huntington. Thomas Sheldon Macon built it as a two-story stone mansion of four bedrooms, a living room, dining room, study, and kitchen. Its big, covered front porch with four large columns was adorned by floral urns and four white wooden rocking chairs with signal quilts hanging on their backs. Quilts had special patterns and would be displayed at night. One signaled, "This is a safe place for runaways." Another pattern said, "It is not safe in this area, so find another location east." Another directed, "West," and another meant, "This whole area is unsafe, so go to Michie Tavern for further instructions." On either side at the bottom of the steps stood tall, black iron hitching posts for visitors to tie the reins of their horses.

Huntington was surrounded by 2,000 acres of beauty, designed with patches of various orchards, plentiful crops, forests, lakes, and waterways, stables, barns with fenced areas for the animals, and the house with its floral grounds to make the most beautiful patchwork quilt.

The humidity was finally gone. The breeze felt good upon one's warm face. The sun shone brightly. Summer was at its end. Mid-September meant harvesting would begin on parts of the land. Huntington soon would be in all its glory. The orchards of apples, pears, figs, cherries, walnuts, pecans, and almonds would be taken care of first. Next, the grapes would be picked, then preserved into jams, wine, and vinegar. The hops would be picked and dried on wire screens, then stored for later to be used. Then, the hay would be made into homey-looking honey golden rolls. The vegetable garden still had some underground items that would be picked and put into the cellar.

The forest trees would change into glorious colors come October when spouts and pails would be placed on the maple trees. Other trees would be chopped for winter fires, cooking, and smoking meat. The animals were assembled and later would have to be put up with each other in the large barn with the attached pastures. In another large barn, horses and mules were housed with access to their pastures. Most of the horses were taken during the war. Thankfully, some of the gypsies, Duke, Lash, and Paddy, helped breed and took care of the remaining horses. This kept the stock growing.

Many of the gypsies helped with the harvest and with storing the crops. In the spring, the gypsies assisted in preparing the soil and planting. In early winter, they would move farther south to warmer weather. While they worked at Huntington, the gypsies had their own campsite between the lake and the forest to park their caravans, or wagons, in a circle. Their families were allowed to fish and hunt in the area. The area kept them safe, as many locals did not like them.

Thomas Sheldon Macon was a widower for seven years. His wife, Hannah, died in childbirth, and so did their son, Jeromy. They had two remaining children, Abby and Matt. Abby was thirteen, and Matt was sixteen at the time of the deaths. Their mother and brother were buried together on a hill under an old oak tree. This would be Huntington's Cemetery. Flowers were placed weekly in vases in front of their tombstones.

Thomas stood tall, had dark eyes and hair, and was attractive, even at his age. He never married again. Hannah was his true love. No one held a candle to her in his eyes. He felt lucky to have Matt and Abby. They were his joy, and he lived for them.

Matt had gone off to war on the side of the Union. His father was the only one who knew Matt was serving as a Union spy. Matt was good at his job. After the war, the president requested he and his partner, John Anderson, stay to do additional secret work. It had been over two years since the war ended. Matt's last letter said he was finally coming home soon. The move home would be permanent. He couldn't wait to see everyone. Matt looked forward to joining his friend, Arthur Howard, at Arthur's law office. It was their dream to be partners in law in Charlottesville, Virginia.

Matt's friend and military partner, John Anderson, was coming home with him. John had lost his family and home in Richmond, Virginia. Matt felt a kinship with John and thought welcoming John to Matt's home would make John feel at peace. Matt also had a secret plan to get John and Abby together.

Besides the Macon family, in a two-room cabin lived Mima Jones, a cook, housekeeper, and freed slave, and her husband, Henry, also a freed slave and an overseer. In another two-room cabin next to the stables lived Joe Jones, affectionately known as JoJo. He was Mima and Henry's son and a stable manager. Sometimes, if the vet, Andrew Turner, was busy until late at night, he would stay with JoJo and have supper with the Macons.

Abby and Mima were laughing as they took down the wash in the back yard. Abby loved Mima like a mother. Mima loved Abby like a daughter. Lying patiently on the ground was a large, black, furry mountain dog named Shadow. Shadow followed Abby everywhere, except when her father accompanied her. That was when Mr. Macon took over protecting Abby. Wherever Abby went, there was Shadow.

Wiping her brow with her right hand, Abby rejoiced, "That should do it for today Mima. I'll go inside and get cleaned up before our guests arrive. We sure did a lot today. Thank you for all your help."

Mima smiled and said, "Once you clean up, help yourself to a glass of cider while you wait on the porch for Miss Mary and Miss Sarah." She laughed aloud. "You all sure have a great time with your once-a-month weekend get-togethers."

Abby laughed, "We sure do. We make such a mess cooking everything for the monthly church picnic, but we do a good job of cleaning up!" Abby sighed. "Too bad it's only once a month."

"Now, scoot!" Mima watched the dark-haired mistress leave with Shadow trailing behind. Those bright blue eyes were her mother's. *How proud Hannah would have been to see Abby all grown*, thought Mima. Mima went off to put the wash away, and then she would finish preparing dinner.

Abby finished cleaning up and grabbed a glass of cider. She and Shadow went out to the front porch. She sat down in the first rocking chair to her right. Shadow lay beside Abby's chair. She placed the glass upon a little table, patted Shadow's head, and looked out. She admired the panorama view she had of Huntington. How beautiful! As she rocked, she quickly fell asleep from exhaustion.

Abby was startled awake by the sounds of an approaching horse and Shadow's growling. To her surprise, it wasn't Mary and Sarah with Mary's father driving up, but a lone man riding on a black horse. Goosebumps ran across her body. Fear shook through her soul. It was the black guard himself,

Mitchell, coming straight to her. She grumbled to Shadow, "I thought Dad and the sheriff warned him to stay away."

Shadow's hair was standing straight up. He jumped up quickly and was ready for action. Abby reached into her pocket for the pistol her father had given her for cases like this. The trauma of the war caused her to keep it close by at all times. She stood up tall, and Shadow stood guard right beside her. They walked and stopped at the top of the stairs to await Mitchell. The black guard sat lean and dark with a mustache. He slowed his horse to a stop by the hitching post.

"Don't even think it," Abby exclaimed in a cool and calm voice. "Just turn that horse around, and don't ever come back!"

"Not until you come with me, Abby," replied a cold, deep voice.

Abby raised the gun and cocked it. "Over my dead body! Now, turn around and leave, or I'll shoot. You know I'm a crack shot. Please leave before I have to shoot, Mitchell!"

They were interrupted by the sounds of an approaching buggy.

"One day, you will be sorry and realize we were meant for each other, Abby," he stated. "I'll be seeing you soon. Have a good day." He turned his horse and galloped away.

Abby's and Shadow's bodies relaxed as the tension was released. Abby uncocked the gun and safely returned it to her pocket. She ruffled Shadow's head. "That was close."

Shadow barked in response, then started to dance in excitement for the guests who were arriving. The buggy approached with Mary, Sarah, and Mr. Frank Tanner, Mary's father, and stopped at a hitching post. Mr. Tanner jumped down and tied the reins to the post. He then helped the girls down and brought down their carpet bags.

The girls hurried to Abby. "Was that Mitchell?"

"Yes. Mitchell doesn't know the meaning of 'no,'" sighed Abby. They both hugged her.

"I thought your dad and the sheriff warned him to stay away from you," Mr. Tanner inquired.

"You know Mitchell," replied Abby, "he is relentless."

Mr. Tanner took the bags inside, up the stairs, and placed them at the foot of Abby's king-size bed. After her mother died, Abby and her father switched beds. Her father couldn't sleep in the large bed alone, and besides, she felt closer to her mother when cuddled under the covers.

Carrying a tray of cider, Mima followed Mr. Tanner out onto the porch. Mr. Tanner grabbed a glass and sat down in a rocker. "Thank you, Mima." He took a sip and winked at her. "Great as usual."

She looked at him and asked, "Was there a problem? You all look white as if you seen a ghost."

"Even worse," replied Sarah.

"Mitchell," Mary added.

"My Lord. That man is the devil himself. Doesn't he know it's no use?" Mima responded. She shook her head, then passed the tray for the other girls to take their cider.

Thomas approached the group on his chestnut horse, hopped down, and tied the reins to the opposite post. Frank got up and placed his glass on Mima's tray. Both men met at the top of the stairs and shook hands.

"Glad to see you, Frank. Thanks for bringing the girls," said Thomas.

"It's my pleasure to bring such lovely ladies together, especially when they are going to cook for the church picnic," replied Frank. Then, he looked out in the distance in search of something and turned back to face Thomas with a concerned look. "Mitchell was just here."

"Damn that man! Sorry, ladies, for my language," growled Thomas.

"Dad, I'm okay. My pistol, Shadow, and Tanner's arrival prevented whatever Mitchell had in mind," soothed Abby as she placed her hand on his right arm. Thomas stared into Abby's eyes.

"I'll have a talk with the sheriff on Sunday. I promise you; next time he is either arrested or dead. Are you sure you're okay?"

"Yes. I was a little shaken when I saw him, but my anger made me strong," responded Abby.

Frank went to Mary and kissed her cheek. "See you girls Sunday. Make sure you make enough for me to eat," he kidded. Frank went up to Thomas to say goodbye. "Well, Thomas, all did go well. Let the girls have a good time now. I must get back."

Thomas turned to Abby. "I'm going to take my horse out back to the barn and cool him down, then get cleaned up for supper. You girls have fun."

As soon as he left, the girls each took a rocking chair, then rocked while sipping their cider and chatted until Mima called them in for dinner. The girls talked with Mr. Macon and Mima's family. They discussed what they were going to make tomorrow. They talked about the new fashion in clothes and hairstyles. When dinner was over, they (and Shadow, of course) went up to Abby's bedroom. There, they talked about who was a good catch, who was marrying whom, and so on. All but Abby had their hearts set on someone. Abby rubbed Shadow's head as they talked and laughed. Abby knew Mary had always been in love with Matthew. He had always loved Mary, but neither expressed their feelings. She still knew that once Matthew was settled, the two would wed.

As for Sarah, she had always loved the sheriff, Charles. Charles and Abby had mutual crushes when they were young—until they kissed. The kiss felt more like affection between a brother and sister. Abby hoped that with more time, Charles would realize that Sarah was a great catch and would marry her.

Abby hadn't found anyone yet. Someday, she would. She could wait. She preferred finding true love over prematurely conforming to societal conventions.

The girls rolled each other's hair in rags and gossiped and daydreamed aloud with laughter.

After midnight, they fell asleep with Shadow, still on guard, sprawled on a rug beside Abby's bed.

Chapter 2: The Birthday Dinner

The girls awoke to the smell of Mima's coffee and honey butter cornbread. What a way to start the day!

After breakfast, they proceeded to soak the chicken pieces in buttermilk. Later, they would bread and fry the chicken. Next, they made the bread dough for rolls and let it rise to bake later. Pie crusts would be prepared and later rolled out once the filling was complete. Each girl then sat out on the front porch with baskets of potatoes and apples, a bowl and knife, and a bucket beside them. They cored, peeled, and sliced both apples and potatoes. Shadow lay beside Abby to take a nap but slept with one eye slightly open, always on guard.

While the girls worked on the apples, Mima took the potatoes to cook and cool for making potato salad in the kitchen. She had cornbread baking. She happily sang a song while working. Once she was done, the girls returned to the kitchen, rolled out the pie crusts, and constructed the pies.

While the pies baked, the girls took the chicken pieces out of the buttermilk, dipped them into breading, then fried them to a golden brown. The smell was heavenly. The pies came out to cool on tables on the back porch. Rolls were now being baked as the last of the chicken was fried.

When all was cooled and ready to taste, Abby gave everyone a plate. Everyone took a little of everything, except the apple pie, which would be saved for church. They went outside and sat in exhaustion in the rockers. Mary took a bite of her chicken and announced how great it tasted. Sarah loved the rolls. Abby loved it all and gave Shadow some bits of chicken. They tidied up their dishes and helped Mima clean the kitchen. No job was beneath these girls.

"You ladies go take a rest before we go to Queenie's birthday celebration," Mima demanded. Lash, one of the gypsy men, was giving his wife Queenie a birthday party. Thomas supplied cider, vegetables, and two large pigs. The girls were bringing Mima's cornbread and a quilt for Queenie that they had all helped make.

That evening, Thomas and Henry got two buggies ready for their trip to the gypsy camp. Everyone was excited. The gypsies were hard workers, fun, loving, and a lively group. Everyone enjoyed visiting. They approached the campsite of twelve Vardo wagons that circled around a large firepit with the two pigs roasting on wooden spits, which men were turning. Music, singing voices, and children's laughter filled the air.

Duke, Paddy, and Lash came up to the buggies to tie the horses up. They then helped everyone down and escorted them to the center. Everyone said their hellos and happy birthdays to Queenie. Mima handed Queenie the quilt. Queenie's face lit up.

"This is exquisite! Thank you so much!"

They sat on wood buckets around the fire. Women passed out plates of food—roasted pork and potatoes and a gypsy stew of carrots, celery, bell peppers, corn, mushrooms, and tomatoes spiced with Hungarian paprika. The meal was delicious.

Mima asked several women their recipes for seasoning the pigs and learned of several new herbs to add to the kitchen. One of the ladies gave Mima a couple of small bags of herbs she wanted. The Hungarian paprika was at the top of her list.

Then, they served plates of Queenie's birthday cake, a dish called Joffre cake. It was a layer of chocolate sponge cake and a layer of buttermilk cake with a center of chocolate cream, then covered with a chocolate glaze. Everyone felt they had died and gone to heaven. It was such a wonderful feast. Once done, singing and dancing resumed.

Vadoma, whose name meant "Knowing One," was married to Duke, another gypsy. She asked the girls to follow her into her wagon. Once inside, the girls marveled at the elegance of the interior. They were impressed by the decorative painted flowers on the wood walls and the beautiful, printed bedspread and pillows. A red scarf covered a white table with four white chairs arranged around it. A colorful Turkish rug lay upon the floor. Lit brass lanterns hung on the walls.

"Please, sit. I would like to read each of your fortunes," said Vadoma. She had long, wavy black hair and bright blue eyes. Vadoma was thin under layers of typical gypsy clothes and headdress. Her large gold hoop earrings gave her a regal look.

Vadoma's long fingers reached for Sarah's hand. She turned her palm up, and with her fingers traced the lines in Sarah's palm. Slowly, she spoke with a Romanian accent, "I see a young man with a star on his chest."

The girls all said, "Ah!" in unison.

"He is tall, handsome, and brave. Your heart aches for him. Don't worry, little one. He will see

your worth and beauty soon. You will marry him."
Vadoma patted Sarah's hand. "Be patient."

Vadoma turned to Mary and spoke softly as she first looked into her eyes.

"Do not be afraid." She took Mary's hand and turned it, so her palm was upright. Again, thin, long fingers traced a palm. "I see another tall, brave, and handsome man. He looks like a soldier." The girls once again gasped in unison. "He has been a good friend for a long time. He will be home soon. He loves you deeply." She paused and ran her fingers over Mary's palm once more. "You will marry next year." She paused again and looked vaguely sad. "On your special day, don't be saddened when someone special can't be there. Know that they wish you much joy and love. You both will be blessed."

She patted Mary's hand. Vadoma turned to Abby.

"Now, for your fortune." She held Abby's palm up and traced her fingers across it. "Oh, my! You are so fortunate. A twin flame is shown in your palm. It is rare. A powerful love is coming your way soon." She paused, sighed, then continued, "The man you will meet will love you deeply, and you him. Yours will be a whirlwind romance. I see that you will marry within a month once you meet."

Vadoma traced more of Abby's palm. Her expression saddened, but Abby didn't notice. Vadoma quickly laughed to dismiss what she saw next. She squeezed Abby's hand.

"A great love comes rarely, but one that comes over and over is special. 'Twin flame.'" Vadoma gave Abby's hand another gentle squeeze.

The girls, now even more curious about their futures, thanked Vadoma and went to find Thomas. The evening was late, and everyone was tired. Once back at Abby's house, they washed up, and as they wrapped their hair in rags, they discussed their fortunes with excited banter. When their heads hit their pillows, they went to sleep quickly and dreamt of their handsome husbands-to-be. Shadow fell asleep on his rug.

Chapter 3: The Church Picnic

Matthew and his friend John left President Andrew Johnson with the promise to return if ever needed. This comforted the president, as he hated to lose his two best men. They loved serving their country, but right now, a civilian lifestyle was the life they chose.

Both men were around six-foot-four, of medium build, with chestnut hair and deep blue eyes. They excelled at their jobs as spies for the Union. Though the war had ended over two years ago, they stayed on to train as many men as possible in the hopes that they wouldn't be needed. From one another, they had learned many different skills. John's favorite story and trick from Matt was what they called "The Sweep." Matt's sister, Abby, would stand still, lean slightly to the side on which Matt was approaching, and raise her arms skyward with clasped hands. At a fast pace, constantly moving on horseback, Matt would drop his reins, lean over, and in one quick sweep, grab her arms, and swing her backward to sit right behind him on the saddle, all while still moving.

It was an ingenious move. "The Sweep" had saved Matt and John in several pinches. Several nights, John dreamt of a young lady with long, black hair, and he did the sweeping.

From John, Matt had learned how to pick locks and hide undetected. John had worked for a Chicago security company called Pinkerton. He'd trained in Chicago, then had transferred to the Richmond, Virginia, office until the war started. One day John received a letter from a neighbor stating that his parents' home had been set ablaze, and that they had both been killed. John spiraled into a deep depression, and it was Matt who helped him get out of it. He talked to John about how much he was needed to help quickly end the war. The neighbor had enclosed John's mother's locket and both parents' wedding bands in the letter in the hopes the heirlooms would give John some comfort. John placed both rings on the necklace and wore it. They would always be close to his heart.

When they were ready to leave Washington, D.C., Matt invited John to stay until spring. It soon would be winter, too cold for home renovations to begin. This would give John time to decide what he really wanted to do next. All was lost. Crops and servants were gone.

They rode half a day to reach Huntington. They brought the horses to the barn to be unsaddled and cared for. A couple of horses were gone, along with the buckboard wagon.

"Shoot! It's Sunday. The second Sunday of the month is always followed by a picnic! Let's get cleaned up and dressed. We'll miss service, but not the picnic," Matt said.

—

When the ladies woke up, the sun shone bright, and the temperature was perfect for the picnic. Sarah dressed in blue calico with matching ribbons in her brown hair. Blue matched her eyes and was her favorite color. Mary was dressed in lavender calico, her favorite color, with purple ribbons threaded through her blonde hair. Abby dressed in pink calico. Her jet-black hair was also done up in matching ribbons and framed her emerald eyes.

The girls helped bring the food out to the wagon, and Thomas carefully loaded the goodies into place. Once done, he spread a protective blanket to cover it all.

"Sorry, Shadow. It's church. You won't be able to come," Thomas said to the dog, who wanted to join the group. Shadow walked back onto the front porch and lay down by the door. Thomas looked at the three excited young ladies. They reminded him of a beautiful bouquet of flowers; lovely, sweet, and special. He helped them up one by one, then jumped up. "Are we ready, ladies?"

They replied in unison, "Yes!"

He flicked the reins, and off they went. Mima, Henry, and JoJo had already packed and gone off to their church and Sunday picnic. The service was quick and the music uplifting.

Once service ended, Reverend Martin dismissed the congregation, who quickly exited. Busy as bees, they unloaded their items and placed them onto the food and beverage tables. Everyone eyed and drooled over the ladies' famous fried chicken, potato salad, rolls, and pies, along with Mima's honey butter cornbread. Thomas set out his barrels of cold cider, then helped bring out more needed chairs. Blankets were spread on the ground for children to sit. Next, plates, silverware, napkins, and glasses were placed at each family table. The girls had dibs on a large table so that all three families plus Sheriff Charles could eat together. No one dared to separate them.

Thomas went to find the sheriff to discuss Mitchell before grace was said. They discussed Mitchell's last attempt on Abby.

"Charles, he is getting to be really bold, and dangerous. We all know that he isn't right in the head and has no control over his temper. If I were there, I may have shot and killed him."

"I understand, Thomas. I'll talk with him. Next time, do what you have to do. He really is getting to be crazy."

"I just wanted you to be aware," replied Thomas. "Thanks for listening. Now, go get some of that delicious food. We have your place at our table ready for you."

The sheriff looked out east and saw two riders coming toward them. "Thomas, did Matt say when he and his friend were coming?"

"Not exactly. Just soon. Why?"

"I think that's them coming our way!"

"About time," replied Thomas as he slapped his leg. He turned and yelled for Abby.

"What's up, Dad?" Abby said, running up to her father.

"Look out east. What do you see?" Thomas asked.

Abby looked and was stunned. Could it be? Her heart began to beat faster. She took off running.

"They're at it again," laughed Charles.

"Yes, they are," Thomas agreed.

Matt and John now had a crowd watching the old familiar scene play out once more. Abby was halfway to Matt when she suddenly stopped. She leaned slightly forward and to her left. Like a sun goddess, she raised her arms together toward the sky and waited patiently.

"John, stop!" cried Matt. "Stay here and watch how 'the sweep' works."

Matt took off racing toward Abby. Abby was a vision to behold. Halfway to Matt, she stood in position, arms still raised to the heavens. John's excitement made his heart beat harder. Matt was racing as fast as he could, headed straight for her. Matt released his reins; the horse knew the routine and recognized Abby. Matt leaned left, and in one sweep, lifted Abby up, threw her behind him, and continued to race on.

The crowd went wild. They cheered, whistled, and clapped at the return performance of Abby and Matt.

John rode toward Matt's father, and Thomas came up to John's horse and introduced himself.

"You must be John Anderson. I'm Matt's father, Thomas Macon. Welcome. How'd you like the greeting?"

"It was spectacular!" John got down and shook Thomas's hand. "It's good to finally meet you. Thanks for having me."

They watched as Matt and Abby came right up to them, then jumped down. Abby hugged Matt so hard, he almost couldn't breathe. Matt was then hugged by his father.

"It's so good to have you safe and finally at home, son." Thomas was nearly crying. "Let's get you men something to eat."

Thomas and Matt walked side by side to the table. John offered his arm to Abby. She placed her hand on his arm, and an unusual tingling sensation went through her entire body. What was it about this man that caused such an intense response in her? Yes, he was handsome, fit, and manly. She thought, *Lord, I need to get control of myself.*

"Hope you're hungry," Abby said, trying to get out of her head. "The church ladies are exceptionally good cooks. There will be so many choices. It will blow your mind."

"I can't wait," John answered. "May I ask what you made?" They stopped at their table, and he faced her. Abby let go of his arm.

"Mary, Sarah, and I always cook together. We made fried chicken, potato salad, rolls, and apple pies. Mima, our cook and housekeeper, made her famous honey butter cornbread," Abby said with pride.

Matthew introduced everyone at the table. All stood in front of their table and waited for Reverend Martin to say grace.

"Dear heavenly father, thank you for so many blessings. Thank you for the wonderful food we are about to receive, friendship, good weather, and especially for keeping watch over Matthew and his friend and for safely bringing them home. Amen."

Everyone responded, "Amen."

"Luckily, I always pack extra plates and flatware just in case. Please take a plate and follow me to the food table." Abby pointed to several open tables. "There is apple cider and water to drink," she added.

Thomas walked up to the girls and informed them that he, the Tanners, and the Vias were going to sit at the Howards' table of three. He left with a plate and flatware in hand. Abby's table was now three sets of young couples. *Is this fate?* Abby wondered.

John had offered to escort Abby to their table. As soon as she touched his arm, his heart raced, and his body yearned for hers. Over the years, he had escorted several young ladies to events, but none ever made him feel so alive. He had to be careful. This was Matt's sister, after all. He needed to keep himself in check.

He was so entranced following the slight sway of Abby's hips that he bumped into Matt.

"That's my sister. If you don't have good intentions, stay away. She is special. Got it?" Matt whispered in warning to John.

"Got it," replied John.

The spread was truly unbelievable, with ham biscuits, chicken and dumplings, herb roasted chicken, fried chicken, ham steaks with gravy, meatloaf, assorted kinds of potato salads, pickled beets, corn on the cob, glazed carrots, peas, all kinds of breads and rolls, applesauce, and several kinds of pickles.

"Where does one start?" asked John.

"My advice is to study the options. Pick out four or five items that strike your fancy. Pick those to eat.

If you're still hungry, go back and pick different ones or more of the same. You may have only seconds. If you're still hungry, don't forget that we have an assortment of desserts," Abby excitedly explained.

John knew what the ladies made, so he picked a breast of fried chicken, potato salad (he saw Abby take some, so he knew which one was theirs), Mima's cornbread, corn, and a ham biscuit. He managed to pile it just right so that nothing fell on his way back to his seat.

The ladies sat at one side of the table as each man sat across from the lady of his choice. The men began eating and made noises of delight with each delicious bite. They raved over the food, especially the tender fried chicken. There was small talk back and forth. Then, it was time for the dessert tables.

The tables were covered with assorted cookies, cakes, and pies. When everyone finished, no one could move. They felt like stuffed turkeys.

There was more small talk, and all in all, it was a great day. The men helped pack up, put chairs back, and clear the area.

"See you back at the house," said Matt to Abby. He gave her another big brother hug. "Love you."

"Love you, too. Don't get lost. You do remember how to get home?" she teased.

"I got here just fine, so I think I can get back just the same. Thank you," he replied. They both laughed.

"Nice to meet you, Abby," said John. "I will see you later."

Thomas and Abby went back home, then unloaded the wagon. Thomas took the horses and wagon into the barn to be taken care of. Abby went into the kitchen and washed their dishes. As she busied herself, she pondered over the day, thinking about Matt's homecoming and the success of the picnic.

Thomas came inside and said, "That was a great day! I'm sure the guys are fast asleep by now. It's been a couple of long days for them." He kissed her forehead. "Now, get some sleep, too. See you in the morning."

"Goodnight, Dad," she replied.

When she was finished with the dishes, Abby walked into her room and was greeted by Shadow. He then curled up on his rug. She was safely home. Now he could sleep. Abby dressed for bed, then jumped under the covers. She thought she heard a harmonica being softly played. The quiet sounds soothed her to sleep. That night, she dreamt about a mysterious man who went by the name of John.

Chapter 4: Cemetery and Mitchell

The weeks that followed were busy with working the plantation and preserving fruits and vegetables. On Sundays, Thomas took Abby by buggy to church while the rest of the men rode their horses. Other than church, Sunday lunches and their evening meals were the only times everyone got together and talked. Life meant early to bed and early to rise. As the weeks played out, Abby swore she could hear a harmonica playing every night before she drifted off to sleep. Its gentle sound comforted her into her dreams.

The day was almost over, and all the chores were done. Abby decided to take Shadow and visit her mother's grave. Mima went to the kitchen to put the finishing touches on dinner. Abby and Shadow stopped to pick a bouquet of wildflowers, which her mother had always loved. She replaced an old bouquet with this new one, in the vase at the head of the grave. She knelt by the graveside with Shadow beside her.

"Oh, mother! Matt is home safe and sound. It's so wonderful. He's brought his friend, John. I think I have feelings for him. It's too soon to tell. The plantation is abuzz with activity. It's the best time of the year. We all miss you."

Suddenly, Shadow stood up and started to growl. Abby immediately pulled out her pistol from her pocket. There was Mitchell, standing twenty feet away by the trees. Abby was ready to shoot, but Shadow raced toward Mitchell. Mitchell shot his own pistol just as Shadow jumped into him, causing them both to fall backward to the ground. They had a strong hold on each other and continued to tussle on the ground. Finally, Shadow managed to bite down on Mitchell's gun arm. As Mitchell released the gun, it went off and grazed Shadow's shoulder. Shadow yelped, but loyal as he was, continued attacking.

Out in the field, John and Matt heard two shots coming from the cemetery. John quickly mounted his horse and headed in the direction of the shots. Matt was close behind. As he approached the scene, John signaled Abby just like Matt did at the picnic. She nodded in acknowledgment. While Mitchell was distracted with Shadow, John sped toward Abby. He released his reins and leaned toward her. In one swift scoop, he lifted her and set her behind him. She whistled for Shadow.

"Don't worry. Shadow's right behind us. Let's get you home."

Abby trembled and cried all the way home. As they approached the house, John yelled for Mima. Mima quickly came out to the front porch. John slid down and carefully lifted Abby into his arms. He was overwhelmed with a protective instinct and so relieved that she was safe. He carried her up to her bedroom. Mima pulled the blanket down. John carefully placed Abby in her bed. To his own surprise, he kissed her. Mima saw what happened but didn't say a word. Instead, she covered Abby and said to John, "You can go now. I'll take care of her."

He didn't want to leave her, but rest was what she needed. He went out to the porch and stood there for several minutes, trying to absorb what had just occurred. His chest was tight. He had unexplainably deep feelings for Abby. He realized that he loved her. He had to find out if she felt the same.

Startled by a horse approaching, John realized that Matt had Shadow lying across his saddle. They headed for inside the barn. John gently took the weak and suffering dog and carefully placed him on a pile of hay. Matt yelled to JoJo to bring soap, water, alcohol, needle, and thread. John reassured the dog that he was going to be okay. John cleaned the wound with alcohol. Shadow didn't move. "Just like in the army, old boy," John whispered as he rubbed Shadow's head. "You'll be good as new in a couple of days. We all owe you big time."

Matt gently lifted Shadow and carried him to Abby's room. There, he placed Shadow on his rug next to Abby's bed.

Downstairs, Thomas confronted John. "He's a bad man. We should round up a posse!"

"He always disappears and never leaves a trace. According to Matt, it's a waste of time. Abby's okay, just a little frightened. Shadow will recover in a couple of days," John reassured.

"She needs Shadow or someone else with her always," replied Thomas.

John thought so, too, and aimed to fill the role.

Chapter 5: Fishing and Mitchell

A week quickly went by with no signs of Mitchell. Soon, the plantation would be at rest. It was early morning, and Mima and Abby had just finished hanging the wash. Nothing else was planned for the day.

"Mima, I'm going to take Shadow to the lake to fish. Maybe I can catch us dinner for tonight."

"You got your pistol?" Mima asked.

"Yes, ma'am," Abby answered.

"Maybe you should take JoJo."

Abby hugged Mima. "I'll be just fine with Shadow."

"If you're not back when everyone else is, I'll be sending someone to get you."

"I hope to be back before then. Come on, Shadow." Obediently, Shadow followed.

Abby dug in the vegetable garden out back for worms and placed them in a jar. She went into the barn for her fishing pole and a bucket. Off they went to catch dinner and relax. Abby stopped and picked a bouquet of wildflowers to replace the old ones at her mother's grave on her way. She sat with Shadow at the cemetery, patting his head while she contemplated the drama of the past couple weeks.

"Oh, Mama," she whispered, "I'm so confused. Matt's friend, John, is doing crazy things to my mind and body. Could this be love? Could he be the one? I wish you were here." Abby cried until she was drained. "I love you."

She wiped away her tears, then she and Shadow stood up and went to the lake, not knowing that the entire time, someone was watching and listening.

Once Abby was out of sight, John stood by her mother's graveside, in front of the fresh flowers Abby had just left.

"I love your daughter. It seems she loves me, too. I hope you approve. Now, how do I convince her? I need to talk to Thomas tonight. I know this is fast, but I just can't wait. I'll take good care of her."

John strode toward the lake. He had much to say to Abby. There he spotted her, standing under a huge old oak tree, fishing pole in hand, line in the water, and with Shadow lying beside her. John stayed in place, studying her admiringly. She was breathtaking. It dawned on him that Shadow wasn't alarmed by his presence in that moment. Did Shadow feel that he was no threat? He started to

71

whistle as he approached her so she wouldn't be alarmed. She turned and smiled.

"Catch anything?" was all he could think of to ask.

"Yes! Just need one more for dinner," Abby answered, flustered at being caught unaware. Shadow got up and approached John. He nuzzled John's hand and then, strangely, Shadow then took off in a run.

"Will he come back?"

"Yes. He likes to sniff around, try to catch me a present," she said, laughing at the idea, "and sometimes takes a swim in the lake. He eventually comes back."

"Like a soldier, making rounds to make sure the area is secure."

Abby laughed at the thought but quickly began to wrestle with her pole. The final fish was caught and put with the others in the bucket.

"It's really such a nice day," she said as she sat against the tree trunk.

"May I join you?"

"Sure."

The trunk was wide enough to support both of their backs.

"Abby," John sighed. He turned his head and looked deep into her eyes. He heard her little gasp of breath. It was a hopeful sign. "We just met, but I feel a strong connection with you. May I hope that you do, too?"

Looking deep into John's eyes, Abby felt his soul and love. "Yes, I do feel the same for you. I've never felt this way before. I wasn't sure what it was until now."

John gently caressed her face and kissed her soft lips. She was warm, inviting, and tasted so sweet. She responded to his kiss, and the affection was heavenly. He wanted more. His right hand cupped her breast. Slowly, he started to knead. Abby moaned into his mouth, but she didn't stop him. He was in trouble. He knew he should stop, but God, he couldn't.

He kneaded her breast until her nipple peaked. *Oh, God. I can't stop*, thought John. His body yearned for her. It was like nothing he had ever experienced. He pressed her lips and teeth apart with his tongue. Somehow, he managed to unbutton her blouse. He lowered it down to her waist. He stopped himself and looked deep into her eyes to ask, "Do you really want this as badly as I do?"

"Oh, yes. Please, don't stop," she replied in desperation.

John unbuttoned her chemise and exposed the nipple that he had wanted so badly to suck. He kissed her neck, then her shoulder. With feathery kisses, he trailed down to her breast. With his tongue, he flicked her nipple until it was so taut that she cried out in need. John laid Abby on the ground. He lay next to her, then leaned over to flick her nipple again and again with his tongue. Finally, to her relief, he happily sucked. His shaft was ready, but he wanted to go slowly. He knew this had to be Abby's first time.

—

Abby couldn't believe that John felt the same. She had kissed Charles once when they were young, but the kiss wasn't what either had expected. It was like kissing a brother or father. To Charles, kissing Abby was like kissing his mother. They decided just to be the best of friends after that.

This was completely different. Abby could see John's eyes were now a deep navy blue. His body exuded heat. When he kissed her, there was warmth that radiated from his body through hers, down to her core. He started to knead her breast again, which stoked a growing need within her. It was a strange and wonderful feeling. Then, he asked if he should stop. She wanted and needed more! More of what, she didn't know, but she trusted him, somehow. He began to suck harder on her nipple. Wetness began to build between her legs, and she felt a need she couldn't explain.

"More," she pleaded.

They heard Shadow barking in the distance. Abruptly, they stopped. John helped Abby button up as fast as they could. Just as Abby sat back up, they heard a horse approaching. Shadow stood next to them. The dog growled as his hair stood straight up. John stood up with his pistol in hand, then Abby stood behind him.

"Well, well, well. Looky what we have here," Mitchell announced sarcastically as he suddenly appeared.

"Turn around and leave," demanded John.

Mitchell raised his pistol. "Who do you think this is for?"

"I can assure you that you are no match against me. Drop the gun, turn around, and don't ever come back," John insisted.

Mitchell cocked his gun, but as John promised, John was faster and shot Mitchell in the shoulder, causing Mitchell to drop his gun.

"Leave now, and I won't kill you. Don't ever trespass here again, or you're a dead man," John spat.

"I guess my timing is off again. I promise not to trespass again, but I also promise that you both will get your just reward. Catch you next time," Mitchell replied and saluted John. He turned his horse and galloped away.

"Why didn't you kill him?" asked Abby.

"I've learned that killing is a last resort. A man deserves a second chance." He turned to her and asked, "Are you okay?"

She started to shake and cry. He held her until she finally calmed down. He kissed her with reassurance and said, "Let's get back to the house."

So, they walked back in complete silence and with Shadow trailing behind. Dinner was delicious but talk was minimal. Abby went straight to bed right after dinner. The men sat to discuss the encounter with Mitchell that day. Then, John asked to talk to Thomas in private.

They went inside Thomas's study and closed the door. Thomas took the seat behind the desk. John couldn't sit, so he stood. Thomas hoped that John was here to ask for Abby. Everyone saw the chemistry between them.

"Thomas, I'm in love with Abby. She's in love with me. I know this is sudden, but I want to marry her as soon as possible before I ruin her. I've been doing my best to be honorable, but it's more difficult than I thought. I'd like to marry her in a week or two. Can I have your permission and blessing?" asked John.

Should I make it hard on the boy? thought Thomas.

He didn't have the heart. He got up and walked around to hug John. "Yes, you have my permission and blessing. Matthew will be leaving about that time to live and partner with Arthur Howard. The plantation will be all set for the winter. Would you consider making Huntington your home? You and Abby can take my room, and I'll move downstairs into Matthew's room. Stairs are getting to be a bit rough on my knees," Thomas offered.

"I can wait two weeks to give Abby time to plan and prepare for a wedding," John said.

"Do you have rings?"

"I have my folks' wedding bands. I'd like to use them, but I need to get an engagement ring."

"I have just the thing." Thomas went around the desk and opened a small drawer. He pulled out a black velvet bag, then handed it to John. "This was Abby's mom's ring."

The gold ring was centered by a heart-shaped ruby with small round diamonds on each side.

"It's perfect," John said.

"How does your dad's ring fit you?" Thomas asked.

"It's just my size."

"Good. Give me your mom's ring. I'll bring it with me tomorrow for Andrew to size for Abby. Every year on her birthday, Abby tries on her mother's ring. It fits her just right. Andrew will make sure your mother's ring fits her just as well. You can have them back tomorrow night. I'll get things set up with Reverend Martin." Thomas hugged John again, then patted him on the back. "Congratulations, son! Welcome to the family."

That night, John was too excited to sleep. He took out his harmonica and softly played as he rocked on the front porch, oblivious to the fact that his music helped put Abby to sleep.

Chapter 6: Engagement and Wedding

John was antsy all Saturday. He and Matthew went riding to oversee the plantation. Little needed to be done. They stopped by rolls of hay. That was when and where John told Matt about his plans to marry Abby. Matt slapped John on the back.

"I knew you two would be a perfect match. I was hesitant at first, but I saw how you protected her from Mitchell. Welcome, brother!" Matt replied. They hugged. Now, John just had to ask Abby that night.

Mima seems happy today, thought Abby. *I guess the cooler weather suits her.*

"What's for dinner?" Abby asked.

"Beef stew, cornbread, and I'm trying the recipe for Queenie's birthday cake," replied Mima.

"All my favorites! You need help with the cake?"

"No. I need to concentrate, and you might distract me. Thanks, anyways. Go do something fun."

"I guess I'll make those rose and lavender sachets for Christmas gifts. I need to get those ready. If you need help, I'll be out on the porch," Abby said.

Later that evening, Abby walked into the dining room. Everyone was quiet, which was odd. Even stranger was how John had been acting the past few days. She thought they were becoming close. Maybe he was the sort of guy who got what he wanted from a lady then left. But Matt wouldn't tolerate anyone like that, so she was certainly confused.

"The dinner was delicious, Mima," said Abby.

"Thank you. Now, you scoot outside while I clean up. Nothing else for me to do tonight. See you in the morning."

Abby went outside with Shadow and sat down on a rocker. She started rocking and was about to fall asleep when Shadow got up to greet someone. It was John.

"Would you care to walk with me before it gets dark?" he asked.

"I'd like that." He offered his arm, and she took it. They walked to the cemetery with Shadow trailing behind. "How did you know my brother and mother are here?"

Shadow lay under the tree.

"I've ridden by here many times on the way to the fields," John answered. He paused, then turned Abby to face him. "I brought you here so I could ask you a question in front of your mother." He held both of her hands, then knelt on one knee. "I know this might seem too soon for you, but not for me. Abby, I love you with all my heart and soul. I never wanted anything so much in my life as you. Will you marry me in two weeks?"

Abby threw her arms around his neck and kissed him with all her might.

"So, that's a yes?" he asked.

"Yes! Yes! Yes!" Abby replied. John pulled out her mother's ring and placed it on her finger.

"I know it's your mother's, but your dad and I thought you would love it," John explained.

"It's exactly what I've dreamed about."

"I have my parents' matching wedding bands. It will make us feel that they are always with us." Then, he undid the chain around his neck and attached it around Abby's. "This was my mother's locket. I wish for you to wear it."

They kissed for a long time. As they went inside, everyone screamed with excitement. They hugged and kissed as one happy family.

Thomas asked, "Is it time for cake?" They all laughed, excited for what was to come.

—

It took a week to get Thomas's belongings downstairs and Matt's things moved to Arthur's house. It took two more days to move Abby into Thomas's old room. Mima's group of friends made the couple a wedding quilt for their bed. Matt and John spent the last three days at Arthur's. John was forbidden to see Abby until they were both at the church on their wedding day.

The ladies from church pitched in on planning the wedding luncheon. Mima had her hands full with making Abby's wedding dress and cake. Mary and Sarah, with their mothers, were in charge of flowers and ribbons. They would decorate the church, tables, and buggy that would take the newlyweds to Michie Tavern for their honeymoon. Unfortunately, Shadow was not invited. He was not happy. He moped and groaned most of the time.

The big day arrived. Mima made a beautiful wedding dress in pale pink silk adorned with tiny white flowers and white ribbons. The cake was made to match. The girls assembled bouquets of wildflowers with long white ribbons. They decorated the buggy with more wildflowers and ribbons. Abby's father gave her ruby earrings to wear that matched her ring, which Abby found to be such a touching gift.

Thomas told Abby she was the most beautiful bride he had ever seen. He helped her up into the buggy. He would ride John's horse back home after everything was over. The birds were singing, the sun was bright, and the weather was perfect.

They parked the buggy by the front of the church. Mary and Sarah were awaiting their arrival with bouquets clutched in their hands. Mary opened the door slightly to tell her mother that everything was ready. The music started to play, and the mothers opened both doors to let the procession begin. Abby's two best friends walked down the aisle with joy in their hearts, and behind them came Abby and her father. All stood up as they walked toward the altar.

From the altar, Matt and John watched the procession on one side of the minister. John hadn't realized he had stopped breathing once he saw Abby, until Matt reminded him to breathe. Abby kissed her father as he handed her over to John. They exchanged vows and rings. The gold bands were engraved with intertwining circles, meant to represent never-ending love. It was perfect.

Reverend Martin pronounced them man and wife, and they were finally able to kiss. Everyone cheered. When it was over, Reverend Martin and the newlyweds stood by the front door as the congregation congratulated the couple one by one. Once outside, more people arrived to help celebrate—Mima with her friends, Duke and all of his gypsy family and their church group. Abby did feel sorry for John. He had no one left to congratulate him, though he did receive a telegram from President Andrew Johnson. In his telegram President Johnson invited John and his new bride Abby to stay with him when in Washington, D.C. He also sent a grandfather clock as a gift, which would fit perfectly in the entrance of their home.

The food was delicious and plentiful. Mima's huge wedding cake was gorgeous and large enough to serve everyone. After the meal, some of the men began to play their fiddles. Adults and children all began to dance. Thomas was eventually able to dance with Abby. Afterwards, he took her aside and said, "It's time to start your new life with your husband. Trust him, work together, and never go to sleep mad. Bless you both." He kissed her forehead and led her to John. "Go quickly, before you're discovered leaving!"

Her father helped her into the buggy, where John was waiting for her. As they started off, a crowd ran after them, throwing flower petals and wishing them the best of luck.

Chapter 7: Honeymoon

The ride to Michie Tavern was long, and parts of the road had sharp curves with steep cliffs. John took his time going up the mountain. Once they reached the tavern, a young lad named Sam took over the buggy. He knotted the reins to the hitching post, lifted the two bags, one in each arm, and brought them to Abby and John's room.

John jumped down, then scooped Abby into his arms and marched into the tavern without putting her down. He intended to walk across their bedroom threshold before he would allow her feet to touch the floor, some type of good luck wedding rule he had heard, and he didn't want to take any chances. They reached a counter in the lobby, where an older woman addressed them.

"Congratulations, Abby and John. We have the honeymoon suite all ready for you. It's located on the second floor and all the way in back for privacy. The door is unlocked. The key is in the lock on the room side. If you need anything, just let me know. I'm Ida."

"Can you send up dinner at about seven tonight, along with a bottle of wine?" John asked.

"Sure. Tonight, we are serving roasted leg of lamb, potatoes, and carrots. Bourbon bread pudding is dessert."

"Sounds great," said Abby. "Are you going to put me down now?"

"Not until we walk over the bedroom threshold!" He took the stairs two at a time, walked quickly to their room, opened the door, and walked over the threshold with his bride. He kicked the door closed. Their bags were placed in front of the wardrobe. "We must tip Sam before we leave. He is taking good care of us."

He lowered Abby to stand, caressed her face, and kissed her softly.

"Is this room to your liking?" he inquired. It was white and decorated in blues and yellows. The large bed had a lovely floral quilt that was folded down for the night with crisp white sheets and pillows. The curtains and valance were of the same colors in a striped pattern. The fireplace was ablaze. Two lit glass hurricane lamps decorated the fireplace mantel, centered with a vase filled with fresh flowers. A blue love seat with a tea serving table was placed before the fireplace. Several landscape paintings were hung, giving the suite a homey feel.

"It's lovely," whispered Abby.

"Not as lovely as you."

John leaned in and kissed her again. She threw her arms around his neck and kissed him with more demand. As he kissed her, he unbuttoned the back of her dress and let it slide to the floor. He broke the kiss and looked into her eyes as he pushed her slip and chemise off her shoulders, letting them also fall. There she stood, in her underclothes alone.

"You're magnificent, Abby," he whispered as he looked deep into her eyes.

"What about you?" she responded.

He quickly undressed to his underdrawers. He didn't want to scare her, and instead wanted to let her get used to him. The first time, one needed to have special care. He had to control himself and pleasure her first. He noticed a washstand with a pitcher of water and towels hanging. They would need that later. Yes, this room was perfect.

He embraced her and felt her body mold to his. He could not hide his arousal. Though naked, Abby wasn't cold. When John embraced her, her body heated up and became alive. She felt his enlarged staff against her. She thought she was wet before; now, she was practically dripping. The sensation there was unbelievable, and it seemed to stimulate her nipples. She was going out of her mind. He kissed her thoroughly, which caused her to moan for more. He lifted her, carried her to the bed, and gently placed her in the center of the bed. He lay down beside her.

"I love you, Abby."

"I love you, too, John."

He leaned over her body and with his tongue, flicked her nipple, driving her insane. She moaned for more, but she didn't know what exactly. Then, he did the same to the other breast. He kneaded then flicked.

"I'm going to taste every inch of you. You taste so good," he murmured.

He removed her underwear and his pants. While sucking on a nipple, he rubbed his palm up and down between her legs.

"More, John, more," she demanded. He moved to the second breast and sucked while inserting his finger. She opened her eyes in shock.

"Relax, Abby. Just feel."

She trusted him. She adjusted to his in-and-out movement, so he added another finger as he sucked. He started kissing down her belly, reaching her womanhood. He sucked her center until she trembled and cried out her release.

"God, Abby. You taste so good. Are you all right?"

"Yes. That was unbelievable!" she gasped.

"We're not done yet."

"We're not?"

"The next part, because you're a virgin, will hurt at first. I'll stop for a couple of minutes, and then we'll start again. It won't be as bad," he explained.

"I trust you. Mima told me what to expect. I'm ready, John."

He kissed her passionately on the lips while kneading her breast. Slowly, he mouthed her breast, then sucked again. Desire returned to her. Sensation was building. He put two fingers into her. She instinctively started to tighten around his fingers, and he pumped. He withdrew them, then carefully placed his shaft at her opening.

"Look at me, love. Look into my eyes when we become one," he said.

She opened her eyes, and as quickly as he could, he thrust deep. She screamed. He kissed her and didn't move inside of her. She needed to get used to him. She placed both hands on his face.

"It was a sharp and quick pain. I'm all right now," she reassured.

He kissed her lips and started to move slowly inside her. They looked into each other's eyes as the sensation built, and they climaxed together. He fell upon her, panting.

"I didn't know how wonderful and special this could be," cried Abby.

He embraced her and kissed her forehead. "Nor I."

He got up and dampened a towel and washed her lovingly. They cuddled.

"Love me forever, Abby."

"I'll love you forever, John."

They fell fast asleep until there was a knock at the door. John covered Abby, pulled on his pants, opened the door, accepted the tray of their dinner, and placed it on the tea table. He stoked the fire and added more wood. He went back to the door and locked it.

"Is that dinner, John?" Abby asked.

"Yes, my love. Are you hungry?" John answered.

"Yes, John, but not for food," she said, stretching her arms out toward him. "Come here. I want more."

"You're going to be sore tomorrow."

"I don't care."

"As you command, my love."

They never ate their dinner. The sun shone brightly through the window the next day. Abby was cocooned with her back to John's front, his arm across her waist. He opened his eyes and smelled their scent. He felt that he was one lucky guy. Abby stirred.

"Good morning, love. How do you feel?" he asked.

Abby turned to face him and planted a quick kiss on his lips. "Good morning, dear. I feel wonderful. A little sore, but not much."

"I'd love to make love to you again, but we should wait until we're home and in our own bed. By then, you won't be so sore."

Abby trusted John, so they would wait. She agreed, "I guess you're right. We have a lifetime to make love."

He kissed her one more time, then got out of bed and dressed.

"I'll be right back with breakfast," he said.

"Hurry back. I'll get dressed and will be waiting for you. It might be lunch time by the looks of the sun. We were up late."

They both laughed. He winked and went to get the food. Abby was dressed and sitting on the loveseat when John entered with a tray laden with goodies.

"It's about four o'clock! After this meal, we need to head out before it gets dark. Especially with the windy, narrow roads," John reported.

They ate almost everything, packed their few clothes, and said thank you and goodbye to Ida. Sam brought the horse and buggy in front. He packed their bags. John gave Sam some coins for all his help, then helped Abby up into the buggy. Happily, they started home. About one-third of the way through their journey, while coming around a sharp and narrow curve, a snap sounded and alarmed John. A shot was fired, which spooked the horse, and it ran. The buggy sped up and became uncontrollable. In an instant, the horse detached and darted away. The buggy rattled as though it would fall apart. Then they spotted the edge of a steep ravine. There was nothing they could do. John embraced Abby and said, "I will love you forever."

He kissed her as they plummeted over the cliff and down the mountainside.

On his horse, Mitchell came around the bend, stopped at the edge, and yelled down, "You could have lived. I loved you, Abby. You didn't have to die!" Tears ran down his face. "He can't love you anymore, nor you, him. You broke my heart. Now I've broken yours."

Alone again, Mitchell turned his horse and rode away.

Chapter 8: Vadoma and the Dark Figure

Reverend Martin led the funeral, and everyone from the community was there. Thomas held a graveside service at Huntington's Cemetery. After the service, all went back to the house except Vadoma and Duke. Vadoma gently dug into the grave to bury a stone heart. Tears ran down her face.

Duke wrapped an arm around her shoulders. "You couldn't tell her this would happen. It would have spoiled all the joy they had," he soothed.

"I know, Duke. I know. It was the hardest thing I've ever done. She and her family have been so good to us all. They are like family to us."

"I know. Paddy said he took care of Mitchell."

"Good. He should have been taken care of long ago, but he was clever."

"Paddy had a hard time finding him. Don't tell anyone about it. We all could get in trouble," warned Duke.

"Don't worry. Just the three of us will know." Vadoma wiped her tears. "They were not just soul mates … they had the deepest love of all. They were twin flames, Duke! They will come back again and again to find each other and start over and over again." She sighed. "I hope one day they will begin as newborns so they can have a long life together."

"Did you see that?" Duke asked.

She turned to face Duke and looked into his eyes. "They will start again. Two broken hearts will become one." She didn't lie. They would always come together again, but she couldn't tell Duke everything she saw.

"That is good, Vadoma," he said and squeezed her shoulder.

"Yes, that is good."

They walked toward the house to mourn with the others.

———

That night, a dark figure cautiously approached and sat beside Abby's grave. The silence of the evening was broken by a soul-wrenching wail. It continued strong for ten minutes. The shape stretched across her grave as though it lay upon it.

Then it spoke, "We loved each other from the beginning. We found each other over and over through time. I knew it was you, the moment I first saw you. I don't think you ever knew it was me. I pray next time we meet, it will be early, and we will have more time in that lifetime."

The figure sighed, closed his eyes, and faded away, snuffed out by a broken heart.

Part III: Never-Ending Love

THE LOVERS

Chapter 1: February 11, 2021

It was Thursday, February 11, 2021. The day began with gently falling rain. The sun was asleep, and almost everyone wanted to join the slumbering star, or at least sleep in a bit later than normal. This would be a lazy day for most. The only other sound was a *tick-tock* coming from the mantel clock above the fireplace in the living room.

Winter in Tellico Village, Tennessee, was unpredictable but moderate in the scheme of its four seasons. Snow flurries came a couple of times, but the snow always vanished in just a day or two. The showers were great for those who loved the snow, but they stopped short of covering the streets and sidewalks for those who detested shoveling snow and salting ice. Most days were moderate and sunny. Light jackets, sweaters, or sweatshirts would do the job perfectly.

Tellico Village had some flat and low areas, but it was mostly hilly. On top of one of the higher hills sat Elizabeth Harris's house. The front view was breathtaking. In the distance spread the Smoky Mountains. The mountains were crowned with a mystic ring of rising clouds like smoke. The view of Lake Tellico made the area more tranquil, especially on sunny days when its blue ripples sparkled like diamonds. The wooded area embraced the house with a homey and protective feel. The wild animals and double rainbows above the lake after a rain brought the power of God to one's heart.

Elizabeth's husband, Michael, was already out and about on his errands. His white hair, baby blue eyes, and tall, Viking frame made him still attractive at the age of seventy-eight. Michael and Elizabeth gave each other trusting freedom but always made time for each other. Though for the last twenty years, their time together was more sedentary. Elizabeth guessed that came with age.

She needed to get up and get ready by 11:15 AM. It had been over a year since the Covid-19 pandemic began. The world had quarantined until a vaccine was developed and administered. Some people were still anti-vaccine, so the pandemic wasn't slowing down as fast as the doctors wanted. Masks, washing hands, and social distancing were all still in effect, but restaurants and shops were starting to open with some restrictions. It had felt like ages since Elizabeth had gone shopping, enjoyed lunch out with friends, taken in a movie or play or concert, played bridge or hand-and-foot or Mahjong, or even served at any of her various volunteering jobs.

During the last year, she had started to hand stitch a quilt for her daughter, Jackie. It was a queen-size log cabin pattern in fabrics of various blues and whites with burgundy center squares. She had pieced the top together and was working on quilting the top, batting, and back together. She hoped to finish by Jackie's birthday in April.

Elizabeth did her stretching before getting out of bed. She stood at five feet, five inches, had a medium build for her age, short hair that shined mostly white with streaks of silver and gray here and there. Her hazel eyes were made up of blue with a golden-brown starburst in the center. If she wore blue, her eyes looked blue, but otherwise, they appeared green.

Her seventieth birthday two days ago was a turning point for her. She considered herself old now but still felt years younger. Her daughter, Jackie, made a delicious Thai dinner for her last Saturday. Elizabeth's two grandsons, Alex and Leo, made her a chocolate cake with chocolate frosting. Everything was delicious. Her son-in-law, Tom, helped cook and cleaned everything up. The family tradition was that the men cleaned up after the woman cooked. The gifts Elizabeth received from her family had a lot of thought behind them, and that made them even more special to her.

All day Saturday, her friends stopped by with their face masks on to deliver special birthday balloons and cards. By the end of the day, she had a huge bouquet of balloons standing beside her white fireplace and birthday cards scattered on the mantel. Her husband's best friend, a widower named Bill, sent a huge bouquet of flowers that made Elizabeth cry with joy. She called and thanked him and invited him for dinner that Sunday. They would eat, then play Mexican Train or hand-and-foot.

Elizabeth turned her head to see what time it was. She had ten more minutes before the alarm was to go off. She decided to stay in bed and think before getting ready. She had been disappointed in Michael lately, especially after not receiving a birthday gift or card from him. It wasn't like him. Their relationship had changed so much.

Elizabeth remembered her first date with Michael Harris. It was her first blind date after graduating college. He was six foot two, had broad shoulders, dark hair, baby blue eyes, black-rimmed glasses, and was well dressed. He was older, but to her that meant he was mature and ready to settle down. What had first infatuated her and made her fall in love with him was a thick curl of dark chest hair that peeked out from his t-shirt. It drove her wild.

He was patient and kind. She wouldn't kiss him until their third date. It frustrated him, but he honored her wishes. Their first kiss was gentle but electrifying. They couldn't believe that they were a perfect match. In six months, they married. Two years later, they had Jackie.

She remembered their first time making love on their honeymoon. It was better than any romance novel she read. She felt she was so lucky to find her soulmate. He always looked at her with loving eyes and could never keep his hands off her.

Things changed two months after their 20th anniversary. Michael had bladder cancer. The surgery was successful, and he had been cancer-free since, but sadly, the illness and treatment resulted in his no longer being able to perform. He was devastated. Elizabeth had tried to explain that there were other ways to please each other, but that just made him more depressed. So, Elizabeth told him that their love for each other was expressed by their kisses, hugs, and helping each other.

After two years, there were no more cuddles, hugs, spooning in bed, or passionate kisses. He had been emotionally destroyed, which in turn destroyed their intimacy. No longer lovers, there marriage became an almost platonic relationship. He even started calling her "Princess." After two years, she started to respond by sarcastically calling him "Papa." He either didn't get it, or he was ignoring it. So, Elizabeth had eventually decided that this was her life now. Just a peck good morning, hello and goodbye, and goodnight.

She cooked and cleaned inside. He washed the dishes, took care of the cars, and tended to the outside. Even their get-togethers with other couples had become less frequent. She had decided that she wasn't going to be lonely. She joined bridge and Mahjong groups, a ladies' group, and did volunteer work. With Covid-19, however, everything was cancelled. She did still enjoy watching her grandsons. She missed sex, but she guessed that a lot of women her age did, too.

Her alarm clock buzzed. It was time to get up, shower, and dress. Her neighbor, Carol, had invited her and two new neighbors, Joan and Martha, out for lunch. It would be great to meet new friends and have a good time. Her three best friends were still too cautious because of Covid-19 to go out for lunch yet. An outing was just what Elizabeth needed. So, she cheered up and got ready.

Chapter 2: The First Meeting

Joan picked everyone up, as she was the farthest down the street. Once Carol introduced everyone, they settled into a comfortable and fun conversation. They were getting along splendidly. The restaurant in town was a small, quaint log cabin. The servers were also hostesses. Happy and with a smile, Kathy greeted and seated them. The menu consisted of southern comfort food and beverages served in mason jars. The group laughed at wild stories and jokes. Elizabeth had needed that so badly. She was glad she had come.

Suddenly, she heard a man's voice beside her table say, "Pardon me, ladies, what's the ruckus about?" First, she saw a pair of navy trousers, and farther up was a navy shirt with police details. Then farther still was a face of a man who was not young, but an older, mature man who was immediately striking. He took her breath away. She felt a spark. Never had she felt something like that before. She looked deep into his eyes. She felt she knew him, but they had never met. Could they have known each other in a previous life? His hair was black with patches of white and cut in a clean crew cut. She wanted to put her fingers through it.

She felt herself blush at the thought. What was she thinking? She quickly looked away and gave her neighbors a look that asked, "What's going on?" They shrugged their shoulders, signaling that they didn't know. Elizabeth looked back at the officer. He hadn't introduced himself, nor had he asked her out or even for her name, but he was intensely staring at just her and was rocking back and forth on his feet, arms still at his sides. What did he want her to say or do?

"We are celebrating birthdays and getting to know our new neighbors," Elizabeth stated. The officer still stared. She blushed beet red and turned to look across the table. No one said a word.

He turned to face them all and said, "You ladies enjoy your day."

Quickly, he walked away. Elizabeth wanted to run after him and ask what he really wanted, but with others around, she chickened out. Instead, she just asked, "What was that all about?"

"Elizabeth, he was hitting on you! I wish my husband looked at me that way," replied Martha.

"No," Elizabeth protested. She felt so naïve. But she was curious. She figured she may never see him again, and this saddened her. The ladies continued to talk for another fifteen minutes, and they agreed to meet up again.

That night, Elizabeth pondered what to do. She needed to know if she was still desirable, if the ladies were right that he was hitting on her, or if the officer had just been messing with her. She decided to go back to the restaurant herself next week and find out. Each night until Thursday, she dreamt of their meeting over and over.

Elizabeth arrived at the restaurant. She was nervous but determined. When he didn't show up by the end of her lunch, she talked to Kathy about what had happened and described the man. Kathy laughed, then explained, "That's the sheriff. He was only joking, honey. He does that to a lot of our customers. He's harmless. He is actually one of the good guys. Sorry if he frightened you."

Elizabeth went home and cried that night over the lost chance at renewed confidence in her attractiveness. For some reason, she felt the sheriff was a link to renewed happiness. She had to get back to reality and cope with her real life. Every night after that, she dreamt of a second meeting with the sheriff when he did care. In her dreams, they were soulmates who had a passionate love affair. When she woke up to reality, she felt worse.

"Pull yourself together, Lizzy. Life goes on," she told herself.

Chapter 3: I Know You're There
May 25, 2021

Three months later, Elizabeth's three best friends, Sally, Mary, and Grace, decided that it was safe to go to lunch together. They would celebrate all the missed birthday lunches. They arrived at the same log cabin restaurant and were seated on the one side of a dividing wall. They caught up on everyone's family events, particularly how each of them avoided going crazy during the pandemic. They laughed and had an enjoyable time.

Suddenly, Elizabeth had an odd feeling that someone was watching her. She looked around. No one was there who she knew. Was she going crazy?

The ladies talked about getting together once a month for lunch and bridge. As they were leaving, Elizabeth said she would meet them at Mary's car; she had to go to the bathroom. As she exited the bathroom, Kathy approached her.

"He was here again. I almost brought him to your table to introduce him to you, but you had company," Kathy said.

"I'm glad you didn't. I really wanted to talk to him alone. Thank you," Elizabeth replied.

"No problem. See you later."

I knew he was here! I felt his stare. We are connected, thought Elizabeth. Had he sensed her? When would they ever meet again?

Chapter 4: The Foretelling Gift
September 25, 2021

It was the end of September. The weather was perfect: mid-seventies during the day and in the sixties at night. Humidity was almost nonexistent, and the trees had just started turning their beautiful colors.

Elizabeth and her best friend, Mary, decided to go shopping, have lunch, and get their tarot read, just for fun. There was a two-for-one $60 special, so why not? Ida Llewellyn was highly recommended online, and she was close to home and readily available.

They had their Christmas gift lists ready in hand. Both were smart shoppers, always looking for a clearance sale or a good deal. The pickings were great today. So much was checked off on their lists. Whatever was left, they would search for online. Lunch was a great reprieve for their tired legs and hungry stomachs. Soup and salad were delicious and just the right amount of food. Their appointment with Ida was at 2:30 PM. They had timed everything perfectly.

Mary drove them through a quaint older neighborhood. They found the address and pulled into Ida's driveway. The house was a small, yellow brick rancher with brown shutters. Short bushes in a row across the front of the house were the only landscaping. The L-shaped cement walkway led from the driveway to the brown front door of the manicured, simplistic home.

They didn't need to ring the doorbell as Ida opened the door to greet them. Ida was in her mid-eighties with long white hair twisted into a bun on top of her head, dark brown sparkling eyes, and a petite and thin stature. Ida wore dark denim skinny jeans and a white sweatshirt emblazoned with large black block lettering that read, "Sorry, I'm Out to Lunch! Come Back Later!"

Mary and Elizabeth both laughed at her sweatshirt.

"My grandson gave me this sweatshirt. I just love it," Ida said. "Please, come in. Go straight into the kitchen. All is set up at the table." Her house was decorated in the colonial style with a yellow, brown, and beige color palette. They sat down on a pair of old-fashioned brown vinyl coaster chairs that surrounded a round oak table. A pile of tarot cards sat on the table, ready to be used. "I'm Ida."

"I'm Mary, and this is my friend, Elizabeth," Mary said.

"It's nice to meet you both," Ida stated, then shuffled the cards. "I'll start with Mary." She laid the top nine cards into a square and placed the rest aside with the bottom card facing up. "These are nice cards. Mary, are you married?"

"Yes."

"I see a happy marriage and family. You and your husband will soon take a trip … near water. It will be a safe and fun trip."

"Yes! We are taking a Caribbean cruise next month. We were worried if it would be safe because of Covid-19," Mary replied.

"You will be safe. Covid-19 will be on a good decline by then. It seems you both need this vacation. After this trip, you will be more relaxed and feel like your old self. I see a major change. Maybe redecorating or remodeling?" Ida continued.

"Yes. We've talked about modernizing our kitchen."

"You will be glad you did and wonder why you didn't do it sooner. Once this is done, watch your spending. Unexpected funds will be needed. I don't see for what, but it will not be for death or anything serious. Maybe a relative needing a quick loan. It will be paid back unexpectedly a little while later." Ida lifted the top card from the pile. "This card represents great joy and happiness in your life. You are one lucky lady. That is your reading."

Ida picked up the cards and shuffled three times. She picked out another nine cards, placed them right-side up in a square, and placed the rest of the deck on the side, with the bottom card facing up.

"Oh, my, Elizabeth! This is an amazing reading!" Ida announced to Elizabeth. Elizabeth smiled at Mary, and Ida continued. "Your life has been full of burdens you have carried without complaint or need for reward. You took them on with love in your heart. This shows you feel so alone, even though you have a lot of love and friends around you. Your past has become toxic to you." Ida's expression became concerned as she spoke. She slowly began to smile again as she continued, "The middle part says the cosmic forces are going to reward you for all you've done. You cannot receive this until you let go of your past. If you don't let go, your future will not change.

Elizabeth looked pensive as Ida moved forward in explanation.

"The last row says the cosmic forces are sending you not a soulmate but a twin flame. He will be a younger person. Don't dismiss him for his age. He's no teenager, but he is younger at heart, perhaps several years younger than you. This will be a great love. The two of you will recognize each other when you meet. If you met already, it might not have gone so well because Elizabeth, you must get rid of your past first, or you will lose him. You will meet again. It's your choice. Do you understand?"

"Yes, Ida," Elizabeth said, her eyes wide.

"You must be the strong and confident person you are. Your last card says you will find another passion in service. It will be a group that helps others. By helping people, you will also help yourself. I hope you both enjoyed your readings," Ida concluded.

"Thank you," they responded together. Ida walked them to the door.

"I wish you ladies a blessed day," she said.

As they drove away, they agreed that their readings were spot on.

"Do you think after all this time, someone will come back into your life? Do you think Ida meant the sheriff?" asked Mary.

"I don't know. I've not seen him in eight months. I don't think it was meant to be. Plus, I am married and committed to Michael. But thank you for a wonderful day," Elizabeth said. She seemed a bit sad to Mary.

That night, just like every night, Elizabeth dreamt of a love she would never have.

Chapter 5: Second Meeting
October 7, 2021

Elizabeth volunteered to take her friend Marsha for her chemo treatment on Thursday while Marsha's husband, Charlie, went for his leg therapy. She would bring the eighty-year-old lady to the room, sign her in, then go to the cabin restaurant to have lunch while she waited for the treatment to end. Enduring Covid-19 restrictions kept companions out of treatment centers. Elizabeth brought her Kindle loaded with a book to read while she dined alone.

Kathy's sister, Cookie, seated her and took her order. Once her beverage and food had been served, Elizabeth opened her Kindle and started to read and eat. It was so relaxing. Halfway through her lunch, she heard someone approach her table. She looked up, expecting Cookie to ask if she needed anything, but was surprised to see the sheriff grinning at her.

"Pardon me. The last time we met, I messed up. I apologize and would like to start again," he said.

Breathlessly, Elizabeth responded, "Please, do."

"My name is James. What's yours?"

"Elizabeth."

"May I join you?"

"Please, do." Elizabeth closed her Kindle and placed it on her bench seat. She couldn't believe it was really him. Her heart beat faster, and she blushed. What must he be thinking? He sat across from her, never once moving his soulful eyes off hers.

"On our last meeting, months ago, I approached your table intending to tease you ladies and make you all laugh some more, but when I looked into your eyes … I lost all thought and couldn't find the right words. I was hoping you would help me out. When you looked away, I felt as though you were rejecting me, so I left. I never gave you the chance to even speak, much less show interest in me. So, here I am to do it correctly. Will you go out with me?" James said.

Kathy came to the table with raised eyebrows and asked, "Sheriff, what can I get you?"

James gave his order.

"You two behave yourselves," she teased, and then she left.

They were silent until Kathy brought his order and refilled Elizabeth's iced tea. Once she was gone, Elizabeth finally had the courage to look at

James and say, "I apologize, too. I misjudged you. I thought you were one of those good-looking guys who thinks all women swoon at your stare and charming smile."

"Not true," James said, suppressing a smile.

"That's why I kept quiet," Elizabeth continued. "The following week, I talked to Kathy about what happened. She said you're just a joker who teases her customers all the time. She also added that you're one of the good guys, and that I shouldn't take offense."

He laughed. "Yes, I do joke around. But when I looked at your face, I stopped. Your face has this angelic glow. I was transfixed, and I couldn't breathe or find any words. I felt something for you I've never felt before, and you didn't seem to feel the same, so I left."

Elizabeth sighed. "I, too, felt a spark I have never felt. Actually, I felt like I'd had met you before. Call me crazy, but maybe in a previous lifetime. You never said my name or did anything to show you were interested, so I looked away and hoped you would go."

"Look, Elizabeth. I'm sorry. I don't have much time. The guys are waiting for me to leave. Will you go out with me?" he pleaded.

"Yes, but let's take this slow. We need get to know about each other," she answered.

"I'll pick you up Saturday at eleven, if that's okay with you," he suggested.

"I'll meet you, as I have errands early that day," Elizabeth quickly responded. It was too early for him to pick her up at her home. For some reason, she could not utter the words that she was married.

"How about here again? It's quiet, and the booths keep conversations private." He hoped that was okay. She agreed, so he continued, "Great. Let's exchange phone numbers just in case something unexpected comes up."

They exchanged their numbers. As soon as he left, Kathy and Cookie were at her table.

"Well, talk!" they cried.

"We were wrong. I have a lunch date with him here on Saturday. We're going to talk and get to know each other," Elizabeth said. The sisters giggled. She didn't have the heart to tell them she was married, and she didn't want to lose their respect. No one understands what goes on in a marriage except the husband and wife.

"He's a good catch, Elizabeth, and so are you. We know you've been lonely for a long time. We can see it in your eyes. I hope it works out. If he acts up, let us know, and he'll have to deal with us!" said Kathy.

"Thanks. I better pay and get going to pick up Marsha."

"Don't worry about your bill. He already paid," said Cookie.

Elizabeth blushed, then asked, "I think he's younger than I am. Is it wrong for us to be together?"

"Elizabeth, at your age, it's not a problem unless you make it. Guys die younger than women, so you'll win out," said Kathy.

"If it bothered him, he never would have approached you or asked you out," assured Cookie.

The ladies went back to the kitchen, giggling. They knew that neither Elizabeth nor James would sleep well the next couple of nights.

Chapter 6: First Date
October 2, 2021

The night before the date James was up most of the night, trying to figure out what to wear. He was so nervous. He wanted to impress Elizabeth with his muscled body and looks, but he felt she wasn't concerned with that so much as she was with his soul, his inner self. But with her blushing, he was assured that she also admired his looks. He ended up picking out a short-sleeved, tight-fitting black T-shirt and snug jeans. *Might as well show off my attributes*, he thought.

He called his friend Carson and talked for a good hour about Elizabeth. Carson said he'd talk to his wife Trish about having a Musketeer barbecue, so everyone could get to know each other, and James would have a reason for a second date. James then fell fast asleep.

—

Elizabeth spent hours with Mary the day before, figuring out what to wear. Once she told Mary of their meeting and the reality of her relationship with Michael, Mary agreed that she should see where the relationship was going with James. They picked out a pair of dark denim skinny jeans and a blue and white floral tunic. Navy sandals, a watch, and pearl earrings completed the look.

Elizabeth sent Mary home at 9:00 PM, as she wanted her beauty sleep. She was so exhausted from worrying all day that she fell fast asleep.

—

Elizabeth walked into the restaurant five minutes early. She was excited to see James again. Kathy came out of the kitchen with two lunch platters and quickly said, "Hi! Let me deliver these. Then I'll be right back." Kathy came back a moment later and released a quiet sigh.

"Sorry, but we've been swamped all day. Love that blouse." She smiled sheepishly. "James is already here. He came in thirty minutes ago. He is nervous. I just wanted you to know, you're his first real date since I've known him. He's an adult, a powerful officer, yet around women, he's like a teenage boy. Be patient and gentle with him. Now, follow me for a surprise lunch."

They walked through the front dining area, then the back area, to a door that went to a covered, screened-in private porch. Kathy opened the door for Elizabeth.

"He's in here. I'll be back with your iced tea and to get your orders." Kathy left, and Elizabeth walked toward their table.

The porch had several sets of tables with chairs. In the center was a table covered with a white tablecloth and a vase of a dozen red roses. Her heart skipped a beat. She looked up to see James looking out the large screen window. His figure demanded attention even without his uniform. Her fingers itched with the desire to run them through his hair.

James had felt her presence before she reached the room. He went to the window to get his emotions and breathing in check. He heard her move to the table and waited for her to make her presence known. How he wanted to rush to her, embrace her, kiss her, and make love to her. The last thing he wanted to do was scare her. Yes, she was a grown woman, but her blushing told him that she was still shy. He needed to go slow until she was ready to take their relationship to the passionate sex he knew they were meant to have.

He smelled her perfume. It had a clean and light floral scent that enhanced his excitement. He took a calming breath, then turned to face her. She was so lovely and radiant, like an angel. His angel. He heard her gasp. Quickly, he walked up to her.

"Thank you for the beautiful roses." Elizabeth said.

"I was told that red roses represented love," he replied in a soft, deep voice. He seated her, and then took the seat across from her.

Kathy walked in with Elizabeth's tea.

"Are you ready to order?"

"Yes," they both replied.

Elizabeth ordered a turkey sandwich with potato salad, and James ordered the Cuban sandwich, also with potato salad.

"I'll be right back with your orders," said Kathy as she promptly stepped out.

"Have you lived here all your life?" questioned Elizabeth.

She found out that his family lived on a street with their last name. His great-grandfather had farmed there years ago. The small town grew when Knoxville city folks ferried across the river to cool off in the summers. Now, there was a bridge to use. On their street, his parents, Uncle William, James, and his brothers' families had built their homes. He omitted how wealthy his family was. He was still cautious about that. He wanted to be liked for himself. It was always an issue with him.

Kathy stepped in with their food and asked if there was anything else they needed, and then she was gone again. James continued to talk about going to Vietnam briefly, getting into the police academy, and running for sheriff. He talked about a high school sweetheart named Sue. She didn't wait for him during the war, and instead married a guy James disliked. When he got home from the service, he concentrated on working on his career.

He was saddened this year by the loss of one of the four Musketeers, Frank. Frank, John, Carson, and he had grown up together, gone into the military together, joined the police academy together, and worked together until Frank and John were promoted at the Lenoir City office and Carson and James were elected to the Loudon Court office. They always met at least once, if not twice, every month on a Thursday for lunch to catch up with private affairs or a laugh or two.

Elizabeth swallowed. It was her turn to talk about her own life. She went through her tight-knit family and how close she and her sister Chris were, even though they lived so far away from one another. She talked about how she met Michael, how he was promoted to Tellico Village, about their daughter Jackie and her family living close by, and how she loved spending time with her grandsons, Alex and Leo. She looked down at her plate, and tears were being held back. She had to be strong. This was one of the hardest things she would ever do.

James sensed her turmoil and said, "It's okay, Lizzy. You don't have to say any more."

Kathy opened the door and asked if they needed anything. James abruptly replied, "No," and she shut the door.

Elizabeth looked up and took a deep breath, then started, "I'm still legally married, but our relationship the past twenty years has been more like a father and daughter." She paused for control, then continued, "My husband, Michael, had bladder cancer. The tumor was the size of a softball. The doctor thought it had spread. After surgery, the doctor was elated that the cancer was self-contained in his strong bladder. He has been cancer-free ever since." She paused again. "With life, everything has a positive and a negative."

She looked down again.

"Go on, Lizzy. I'm here for you. I'm not going anywhere. I need to know all of you," James reassured her. Calling her this endearing nickname felt right.

"After his six-week checkup, we were able to get back to having sex, but ..." She looked back up to watch his response, "... he couldn't perform. He talked to the doctor and was given medication to take, but to no avail. It was hard on him, on both of us. I lost my best friend, my husband, and my lover that day. It was just a peck good morning, hello and goodbye, and goodnight. He did his stuff, and I did mine. I joined groups to compensate for my loss. I started to hand quilt to take up more time. I read a lot of books. Only my sister and my best friend know. I've been by his side during several surgeries and a mini stroke."

She took a deep breath and then continued, "In all our married years, I never thought to betray our vows until I met you. I was content and happy with the life I had. I believe he cares for me and still wants to take care of me, but like a father. He even started calling me 'Princess.' When I met you, there was a spark, and I became alive again. I wanted more than the life I was living. I won't divorce him until I know there is more for me. Is this wrong of me?"

She looked back down at her plate. James got out of his seat to embrace her. He lifted her out of her chair. He lifted her chin up with his hand and looked deep into her eyes.

"I know you won't let me kiss you yet, though I want to so badly." He hugged her as she cried her soul out. He whispered in her ear, "I'm here for you in the long run, Lizzy. I'll never leave you."

She finally calmed and said, "I must look a mess."

"You will always look perfect to me." He leaned over to pick up a napkin, then dabbed it in water. "Just a little mascara damage and red eyes," he said as he cleaned her face. "That's better. You can escape any prying eyes by using the back porch door, but first, I need to say, I love you, Lizzy. More than ever. I understand your situation, and I will not run away. I'm here for us. Us, Lizzy." He took a deep breath and looked deep into her eyes. "I'll call you tomorrow to set up our second and third dates. We need to make it real soon because I really need to kiss you."

Her tears were drying as she listened to his words. When he was done talking, she punched his shoulder and said, "You are a joker. Thank you for understanding."

"You are one of a kind. Someone else would have had lovers all those years or divorced him. No,

Lizzy. I'm not going anywhere. I know we just met, but I know in my heart that you're mine forever. Now, take your flowers and go home. Get some rest. This has taken a lot from you."

He handed her the vase with the flowers and her purse with her attached keys. She blushed, thanked him, and then left through the back porch door.

James sat down. That was not how he expected things to go. How was he going to convince her? He wished he could have a heart-to-heart talk with his father. Being Catholic was sometimes hard. This was a bad situation in the church's eyes. His mom would be out shopping with friends, so now would be a great time to get his father alone.

First, he would pay the bill. He was sure the girls would want to know what happened. He would just say it went great and he had to think about where to take her for another date. That should be enough information to keep them happy. So, off he went.

—

Elizabeth had to talk with Michael. She couldn't date James behind his back. Michael was reading a book in his recliner. She put the vase on the kitchen table. Standing beside Michael, she started to speak.

"Michael, we need to talk." Michael put down his book and looked up at her. She continued, "I've met someone today. I'd like to date him to see if it is something special. You and I have not been close these past twenty years. I feel like your daughter, not your wife. We don't hug, cuddle, or do anything passionate. I need more."

Tears welled in his eyes.

"I didn't realize. I guess I've been so self-obsessed. I do love you," Michael said.

"It's not the sex, Michael. There is no tenderness anymore."

"I'll set up a visit with my sister for two months. When I get back, we'll discuss whether you stay and work things out or leave. I'll do whatever you want. I do want you to be happy, Princess."

She really appreciated him giving her space. "Thank you, Michael. I am sorry."

"I know, Elizabeth. I'll leave tomorrow morning. Take care," he stated with no emotion.

Chapter 7: Father and Son Talk and Sister to Sister Talk

James pulled up to his folks' home. The window was open, and he could hear the TV was on the Game Show Network. His dad loved game shows, and his mom loved to shop. He didn't need to ring the doorbell; the door was always unlocked. He walked in, and to alert of his presence, he yelled, "Dad! Are you home?"

His dad came from the family room, then hugged James, greeting, "It's good to see you. Want something to drink?"

"No, I'm fine," James replied and looked his dad in the eye. "I need to talk to you about something personal."

"Come into the family room and have a seat." James's dad clicked off the TV and sat in his recliner. "So, talk."

"I found someone special."

"About time," Jimmy said as he reached over to slap his son's leg.

"We met in February, but I botched it up. With Frank's death and work, I forgot about her until a week ago when we met at lunch again." James took a deep breath and slowly let it out. "I think she's a little older, but that doesn't matter to me. When I looked into her eyes, my heart raced, I couldn't think straight, and believe it or not, she glows like an angel to me."

"What's she like?" Jimmy asked.

"Her name's Lizzy. She's sweet. She's shy, but forces herself to be outgoing. She even blushes." James looked to the heavens for help on what to say next. "She is still married but has been faithful to a man who's more like a father than a husband to her until she met me. Now, we want to see if we can work it out before she divorces her husband."

"Wow!" Jimmy ran a hand through his hair. "You sure about her? The Catholic church has become more liberal on divorce, but are you sure about making a commitment with her for the rest of your life?"

"Yes, I am. I know I just met her, but Dad, the feelings are so strong. I want to marry her as soon as she's divorced. I know I need to give her time to make sure what she wants. I need for us to really get to know each other, too," James answered.

"That's what I'd advise you to do. Give it two or three months to get to know each other. If she makes you happy, it's all right by me. I'd sure like to meet her. I don't know about your mom. She's still hopeful you'll find a young thing, marry, and have kids." Jimmy held up a hand. "I know. You love kids. But because of Vietnam, you can't have any. Did you tell Lizzy?"

"Dad, at our age, getting pregnant is no longer an issue."

"You still need to talk about it. To change the subject, your niece, Vickie, just got engaged. There'll be an engagement party in a couple of weeks. Ask your mom if you can bring someone. She'll perk up until she meets Lizzy. She only wants you happy," Jimmy said. He got up and gave James a hug. "You take care and just be sure before you jump into anything."

"Thanks, Dad. I love you."

"I love you, too."

Just as James got into his car, the phone began to ring. He answered with, "It's James."

"Hi, it's Carson. The barbecue is on for Saturday at 11:00 AM. Everyone can't wait to meet Lizzy."

"Thanks, Carson. We'll be there. I'll see what Lizzy wants to bring," James replied.

"Sounds good. Just let Trish know. You know how she likes no duplicates," said Carson.

"Okay. Talk to you later."

James hung up and dialed Lizzy's number.

"Hello," she greeted.

"Hi, Lizzy. It's James."

"Only my family members call me Lizzy. I like hearing you call me that," Lizzy responded.

"Elizabeth is too formal, and you're much too fun for that," he replied.

She laughed and asked, "What's up?"

"We've been invited to the Musketeers' barbecue at my best friend Carson's house on Saturday at 11:00 AM. Are you up for it? If so, what would you like to make?" James asked.

"I'd love to meet them. I'll make potato salad. How many people do I need to make it for?" Elizabeth answered.

"Eight, maybe. Should I pick you up or meet you somewhere?"

"You can pick me up at my house. Michael will be out of town for two months to give me time to work things out."

"Just text me your address. I guess I'm not ready to face him, either, but I would if I had to," James said.

"By the way, next Sunday, my daughter has invited us and some of my couple friends to have dinner and get to know each other," Elizabeth said.

"That sounds great. We are getting to be popular," James replied.

"Is 5:30 PM okay?"

"That sounds great. Text me your address, and I'll see you Saturday."

James texted Trish about the potato salad, which was great by her. He was glad that Michael went out of town. It would give them a chance to see how perfect they were for each other. He was sure Michael wouldn't deny Lizzy anything, either.

—

That night, Lizzy called her sister, Chris. She poured her heart out, leaving no details out. Chris loved Michael. He was a great guy, but not much as a lover. Chris reassured her sister that all would go as it should, and that everything always worked out right in the end. They caught up with their families. Before they got off the phone, Lizzy agreed to call again later with more updates.

Chapter 8: Second Date – The Barbecue
October 9, 2021

James arrived at 10:30 and was surprised by the Halloween decorations outside. The doorbell, when he pressed it, made a haunting sound. Lizzy answered it with a smile that was anything but scary. She was a joker just like him. He felt at ease with his quirkiness. She answered the door in jeans and a black T-shirt with a large witch's hat in the center that read, "Bad Witch!"

"Am I dressed okay for the barbecue?" Elizabeth asked.

"Yes, you're perfect," James reassured.

"Come in while I get the potato salad out of the refrigerator."

The exterior of her house consisted of a stone front with green shutters in a cottage aesthetic. Inside was decorated in a casual country French style with quirky accents here and there. A place kids would love, and adult would feel right at home: comfortable and welcoming at the same time.

"You have a lovely home," James remarked.

"Thank you. Would you like to see the quilt I'm working on?" asked Elizabeth. James agreed, so she handed him the bowl of potato salad to hold while she unpinned the quilt and spread it across the living room sofa and coffee table. "Don't mind the mess. I hand quilt while watching TV."

Everything she needed was spread across a narrow side table next to her chair.

"This is amazing! You're doing this all by hand?" James praised.

"Yes. My two fingertips are a little numb because I don't like wearing a thimble or pad." She turned the quilt over to show the back fabric pattern of fireworks in various colors. "I made it reversible. Jackie can use it either way. We better get going."

He followed her out to the car. Once she buckled up, he handed her the bowl. It was at that point when he finally noticed the Halloween decorations on top of the potato salad. Hard-boiled egg eyeballs, carrots with green olives for fingers, and black olive spiders.

"This is really cute," he said.

"Thank you," Lizzy said, blushing of course.

On the drive, he reassured her that everyone would be friendly and would love her. He told her their names and who was married to who except for Alice, who was Frank's wife.

"I'll be lucky just to remember Alice, Trish, and Carson's names," she said.

"Do you want to be called Elizabeth or Lizzy?"

"You pick."

"Lizzy it is."

They pulled up to a small red brick ranch with black shutters. Lizzy followed James around to the backyard. She found everyone in jeans and T-shirts. She finally relaxed. Two picnic tables were pulled together and had been covered with a Halloween-printed tablecloth. A long white folding table held plates, flatware, and food. Under the table were two coolers, one with beer, and the other with water and canned soft drinks. A large grill was smoking and whatever was on it smelled delicious. James gave Lizzy a water, and he took a beer.

After introductions, the men huddled around the grill, and the women gathered around the food table. Trish complimented Lizzy on her spooky-looking potato salad. They all made her feel welcome by telling her hilarious tales of James and the rest of the Musketeers. Lunch was delicious. These women certainly knew how to cook. Lizzy was happy when the men took seconds of her salad. As they were leaving, everyone told Lizzy they were so happy that James had *finally* found someone wonderful.

On the drive back to Lizzy's house they recalled everything that happened at the party, and laughed together. Suddenly, it was announced that James's mother, Marcy, was on the phone. He put her on car speaker and let her know that Lizzy was in the car with him.

"Oh, good. I wanted to invite both of you to Vickie's engagement party next Saturday at 6:00 PM," Marcy replied.

Lizzy nodded but was too shy to speak.

"Yes, Lizzy and I will attend. I can't wait for you to meet her," James said.

"It's Sunday-dress casual. See you both then. Bye."

James pulled up in Lizzy's driveway, and turned the engine off.

"I hope you're up for meeting my family. My mother can be a bear at first, but after she gets to know you, she'll be just fine. I promise after next weekend, we will have alone time," he said.

"James, I'd love to meet your family and for you to meet mine and my friends, but I can't wait for alone time either," Lizzy replied.

He walked her to the door and said, "Next time is our third date. I can't wait to kiss you." He handed her the empty bowl where the potato salad once was.

"Thank you for today. I had a great time. They're a wonderful group. Do we need to get a gift for Vickie?" asked Lizzy.

"It is already taken care of. My sister-in-law has the four of us going in on something. I've already given her the money and signed a card. I got it covered. I love you, Lizzy," James answered.

"I love you, too. I'll be busy this week with my grandsons. They have fall break. So, I'll see you Saturday."

Chapter 9: Meeting the Family
October 16, 2021

For the engagement party, Lizzy wore a black pantsuit with a printed black-and-white blouse underneath and black flats. She was anxious to meet James's family. He arrived wearing black slacks and a long-sleeved black shirt. He handed her a bouquet of mixed flowers, which she put in a vase of water and placed on her kitchen table.

"Don't worry. Everyone will love you because I do," James soothed.

They arrived at the backyard party five fashionable minutes late. A long table was set up with assorted appetizers and finger foods. Another had desserts and sweets, and another table served wine, beer, soft drinks, tea, and water. Assorted white and gold balloons were the simple decoration. Everyone seemed excited to meet Lizzy, which helped her relax. There was soft listening music playing on a loudspeaker outside. The engaged couple were bubbly and happy. His parents greeted Lizzy with hugs and excitement, as did the rest of the family. All was going well.

James led her to a dancing area and pulled her into his arms. The song "Stay" was playing. They looked into each other's eyes. It felt so right and wonderful. They were in their own world for two more dances before James's mother, Marcy, interrupted them. Marcy asked James and his brother to go home and pick up more ice cubes. She seemed to have underestimated.

They left and would be back quickly, as they all lived down the block. Marcy turned to Lizzy and said with a stone face, "You seem to be a lovely person, Elizabeth, but you're too old for James. What are you thinking? What is he thinking? And you're still married!"

Lizzy blushed this time because she was so embarrassed. She was also a little angry at this intrusion. This was not what she had expected. Suddenly, Jimmy joined them.

"Honey, we're almost out of your crab dip. Do you have any more?" Jimmy asked.

"Of course. I'll get it and be right back," Marcy said.

Jimmy looked at Lizzy. Yes, she was about eight years older than his son, but she was a wonderful person. She didn't deserve the whiplash Marcy gave her.

"Sorry for my wife's biting words. I can't imagine what she said, but I can assume it wasn't pleasant. Once she realizes how much you two are in love, she'll come around. I promise," Jimmy reassured.

"I don't think so, but it was nice of you to say. This isn't going to work," Lizzy said as she turned to leave, keeping the tears at bay. Jimmy put his arm around her shoulders to stop her.

"Don't go. She will come around. Trust me. Don't you love my son?"

She hugged him, about to cry, and replied, "I do."

"Then don't let that ninny break apart what is good between you two. I've seen the looks you and James give each other. All the affection. It's in your eyes, pure love. I'll protect you from the big bad wolf," James promised. They both laughed. Lizzy gave him another hug, then released him. He was such a dear old man.

"What is this? Is my dad making moves on my girl?" laughed James.

"I tried, but she wouldn't have me. Guess I'm stuck with Marcy," Jimmy joked. They all laughed. James handed his dad the ice.

"Are you okay?" James asked.

"Yes. Your dad is sweet. He just reminded me how much I love you," Lizzy replied. James kissed her in front of everyone. He didn't care. It was soft and quick, but it sent sparks through their bodies. They enjoyed the rest of the party as Jimmy, true to his word, kept Marcy away from the lovebirds.

As James drove Lizzy home, he had to ask, "What happened with my mom? I know her, and I'm glad Dad stepped in."

"She doesn't approve of an old lady dating her son," Lizzy said.

He abruptly stopped the car, then pulled over. With hands clutched to the wheel, he continued, "I'm so sorry, Lizzy. I hoped with everyone around, she'd behave."

"Don't worry. Your dad said she'll come around. It just hurt to have her say that I'm too old."

"You're not too old. Men tend to die off before their wives, so we're just right." At his joke, Lizzy laughed. He started the car, turned it around, and instead of driving toward Lizzy's house, he drove toward his own. "I want to show you how old you are in my mind."

He touched the garage door opener a block away so he could just pull into the garage. Once in, he pushed the button again to close the door.

"Stay here. I'll be right back."

He went straight into the house and directly to the front door, deadbolted it, started taking items out of his pockets, took his gun off, and went to the kitchen table to set it all down. He wasn't going to be interrupted by anyone. Quickly, he went to his bedroom and rolled down the quilt. Thank God, he had just washed his sheets. This is what he had wanted to do since he first met Lizzy. He opened the car door and helped her out. He slammed the door with his hip as he lifted her into his arms.

"I'm practicing carrying you over the threshold," he said, gently bouncing her. "Either you need to lose a little weight, or I need to gain some muscle."

They both laughed. He took her across the threshold, then nudged the door closed. Quickly, he walked to the foot of his king-sized bed and slid her down the front of his body. He hoped she would feel his want of her, and she did. Gently, he cradled her head in his hands. He kissed her softly, then more intensely. Suddenly, she stopped kissing him. Lizzy panted as she stared into his eyes.

"I want this, too," she said.

It was all he needed to hear her say, but he needed to tell her his secret before they went any farther.

"Lizzy, when I was in Vietnam, I was captured and tortured," he began. Sadness showed in his face. "I have physical wounds in several places, not too bad ... but they castrated me for fun."

"Oh, James. It's all right. We don't need children at our age. You can share Jackie, Alex, and Leo." Then she realized there might be more. "What else?"

"I was lucky in the sense that I'm still fully functional. I just shoot blanks," he joked with a smile.

"I guess we don't need condoms," she joked back. "Is there anything else you'd like to tell me?"

"No. I stopped having nightmares a couple of years after I got home. I've not gotten serious with anyone. I know most women want to have their own kids, and I didn't want to disappoint anyone, so I never got serious. Only my dad and buddies know."

Lizzy kissed him with all of her soul. James tugged off her blazer, lifted her blouse off, and continued, "You're beautiful, Lizzy." She did her adorable blush. He unhooked her bra and slid it off. "All-natural and just my size."

"It's your turn," she laughed as she unbuttoned his shirt and slid it off. They hugged and kissed as their passion built and their bodies cried for more.

"We have too much on," Lizzy complained as she pulled her pants and underwear down in one swift move. She kicked off her shoes and stood. "Your turn."

He quickly finished undressing and teased, "Was that fast enough for you?"

"Not really." She blushed again.

He stood before her and palmed one breast, and with his other hand, he palmed her womanhood. She moaned with pleasure into his mouth. He took one finger and entered her. He felt her tighten around his finger. It felt so good already. He spread her legs wider apart, then added a finger. Her hands grasped his head and ran through his hair as she had always wanted to do. She moaned again, and it excited him. He started to finger pump her until she screamed her release, and his fingers were wet.

He gently lifted her and placed her on the center of his bed. He climbed over her and centered himself between her legs. He placed his tip at her entrance, then sucked on her nipple while using his hands to massage the other breast. Then, he switched.

"More," she cried out, so he slowly entered her. She had to be tight like a virgin after no sex for twenty years.

Lizzy couldn't believe how wet she became. He stirred things in her that she hadn't felt in years. She wasn't embarrassed climaxing on his fingers. What would it be like with his manhood? As his tip rested against her, the need intensified for him to be inside of her. Was that her moan or his? He was finally fully inside of her. It felt so wonderful.

"Lizzy, look at me. I want us to watch each other as we climax together." James began to build up speed until all their nerves hit peak sensation that made the heavens explode. They had released just seconds apart. James collapsed on top of Lizzy.

"I've no words to describe what happened. That was a holy experience," he whispered between ragged breaths. "I'll be right back."

He came back with a wet washcloth and dry towel. He lay down beside her, then he gently cleaned her. Next, he threw the towel on the floor.

"I love you, Lizzy, until the end of time." Then, he kissed her.

"I love you until the end of time, James." She slid her back into his front, and he embraced her. Happily, they fell fast asleep.

Chapter 10: Jackie's Dinner Party
October 17, 2021

Sunday was bright and a little chilly at sixty degrees. James had showered, dressed, and was in the process of making breakfast. Coffee was already brewed and filled the house with its aroma. He never slept past six, but today he had woken up at eight. He hoped the dinner at Jackie's would be better than last night. Elizabeth's family could feel the same about him, but in reverse.

Lizzy woke up to the smell of coffee and an empty bed. The smell of bacon forced her out of bed to dress. It would have to do until she got home to shower and change for Jackie's. She stood at the entrance to the kitchen from the hallway. She drank in the handsome man who loved her. She admired his singing while he prepared their breakfast. She loved a man who could cook. She loved cooking, but it was always a treat and a show of affection when a man cooked for a woman.

"Smells delicious." She walked over to him. He turned, and they kissed. "I'm starving."

"Good. I hope you like bacon, scrambled eggs, and toast. Coffee, tea, or orange juice?" he asked. "Hash browns will be ready in just a minute."

"You're making a breakfast the size of Texas," she replied.

He handed her a mug of black coffee and asked, "Need anything in it?"

"Just plain, thank you," she responded, then sat down and waited to be served.

They ate breakfast quietly and gave each other loving glances. They cleaned up the kitchen together, then left for Lizzy's house so she could get ready for Jackie's dinner. She turned the TV on and flipped the channel to a football game that was in progress. It was nice to see James relax at her place. After an hour of prepping, Lizzy walked out with black slacks and a beautiful, printed tunic. He got up and came to her. They hugged and kissed, and he said, "You look beautiful as always."

"We have time to finish the game. Do you want anything to drink?"

"A beer if you have one, no glass. If not, just water."

She came back and handed him a bottle of beer and sat her iced tea on the coffee table. She sat beside him on the sofa, and he put an arm around her.

"We can pick up some flowers on the way to Jackie's. Let's just relax," he suggested. It was nice to simply exist together. As they pulled into Jackie's driveway, her three friends with their husbands pulled up one car after the other behind them. James helped Lizzy out of the car and handed her the flowers. They walked to the first car where she introduced James to Mary and Curtis, then Sally and Rick, and finally Grace and David. They seemed to already accept James. When she introduced James to her family, her grandsons wanted to know where their Papa was. They explained that he was visiting his sister, so Nana brought a friend. The explanation ended their curiosity.

Jackie made lasagna, garlic bread, and a tossed salad. Questions were asked about James, and he in return asked questions about everyone else. Some stories of Lizzy were told, while the men then talked among themselves about fishing, golf, and football, while the women talked about their kids. Lizzy helped Jackie clear the table for dessert. In the kitchen, after Jackie made coffee, she turned her mom to face her and said, "Mom! He's gorgeous and so kind. He looks at you the way Dad used to. I have to admit, I really like him. I think everyone does. I know Dad hasn't been the same toward you for years. I'm sorry. I hope this works."

She hugged her mom.

"Thanks, Jackie. It means a lot. If things were different with your dad, I never would have accepted going out with James," Lizzy replied.

She took the tray with the coffee, and Jackie carried in the cheesecake.

"Let's get this party back on track! Cheesecake, anyone?" yelled Jackie.

The evening went better than expected. Lizzy's friends corralled her before they left to say they were happy for her and that they loved James. It was a bonus that he was candy for the eye.

As they pulled away, James asked, "Lizzy, I know it's early, but I would like you to move in with me. You will get to know all my faults, and I know you don't have any."

She laughed. "Yes, I do. I think that's a great idea, though. We need to stop at my place so I can pack a few things up now and get more later in the week while you're working."

Lizzy quickly packed all her basic needs and a suitcase of clothes. She handed James a few coats, jackets, and sweatshirts for him to carry. She bagged a few pairs of shoes. Back at James's house, he unloaded everything.

"There's plenty of room in the big walk-in closet. I don't have a lot. These drawers in this dresser are empty. All my stuff is in this one. Arrange however you want to. I can adjust," James said.

"I'll unpack tomorrow while you're at work. Tomorrow night, we can get my car so I can do some running around later. I just need to unpack this overnight bag, then my toiletries and medications."

"You go ahead. My stuff in the bathroom is on the left side. Luckily, there are two sinks and sets of drawers. I'm going to prepare a surprise for you. It should be ready in five minutes." He started toward the bathroom when Lizzy stopped him and handed him a duffle bag of toiletries and medications.

"Please put this on my side of the counter. I'll work on it later," she said.

"Sure." He kissed her and left.

It took only five minutes to put the few things away. She was on her way to the bathroom to unpack her toiletries when James came out. He kissed her, then led her into the bathroom. In his large spa tub he had drawn a bubble bath, and candles were set around it. He explained, "It is one of my fantasies to bathe you and have sex in this tub."

"How can I say no?" she said in delight. All of this was crazy, but it felt so right.

Chapter 11: Mary's Birthday Luncheon
October 28, 2021

Lizzy and James enjoyed their evenings living together. After dinners in the evenings, they either shared quiet time for watching TV or reading, unless romantic music and dancing lead to sex. Some evenings, dinner was ignored, and sex was the main course. Who needs food? Some evenings, it was back and foot massages, followed by a spa bath. Every moment together counted.

Thursday, October 28th arrived. Lizzy planned a special birthday luncheon for Mary with Sally and Grace. She made a crab quiche, fruit salad, and a carrot birthday cake as requested by Mary. They would play bridge, eat, open presents, and talk. James brought mixed fall flowers to put on the kitchen island as a centerpiece. Lizzy placed the plates and wrapped flatware on the left side of the flowers. Later, she would place the food on the right side. The kitchen table was set with cards, a score pad, and a pencil. The counter next to the refrigerator had an assortment of beverages and glasses.

James left early that morning for work. Lizzy thought about how helpful and caring James was in helping her prepare for the luncheon. He didn't mind her faults, and even helped ease some of them. She didn't mind his faults, either. She noticed his twin personalities. One was his lighthearted, easygoing, and mischievous nature. The other was his professional side, his quick-thinking strength and overpowering force. It was this side that scared her a little.

The doorbell rang which brought her back down to reality. The girls had arrived and were ready to have fun. They hugged, put presents on the coffee table, and took a quick tour of the house. They loved the clean, modern look of James's home and noted "Lizzy touches" here and there.

Quickly, they selected their beverages and sat to play bridge. They talked about what was happening in their lives. Lizzy assured them how happy she was and that she had made the right decision. They all agreed, for it showed.

They enjoyed the delicious food. Mary opened her gifts and loved them all. They promised to get together after Thanksgiving with Mary hosting. Lizzy closed the door after they left and sighed. She felt at home. Now, to get cleaned up and dinner ready for James.

Chapter 12: Halloween and the Musketeer Girls
October 30 and 31, 2021

It was Saturday morning, and Lizzy went with James to help the officers prepare for the Halloween parade in town on Sunday. They had lunch out, then came home. Lizzy invited Alice, Trish, and Becky for a casual dinner and cards, while the men worked the Halloween events and did extra patrolling. Lizzy kept the menu simple with chili, honey buttered cornbread, and apple pie with vanilla ice cream. She made sure she had enough for the guys to eat as a late snack. Beer, soft drinks, iced tea, and water filled the refrigerator.

Once all was done, they ordered pizza to eat while watching football. The game was still going, but the pizza was all gone. James had a better idea than watching football. He got up, lifted Lizzy into his arms, gave her a wicked smile, and went straight to their bed.

He stood her up beside the bed and undressed her, then himself, as he teased, "I have better entertainment planned."

He kissed her passionately while kneading one breast. His other hand spread her legs, then fondled her opening. She was so wet already. His mouth trailed kisses down to the kneaded breast, and he suckled it like a baby.

"Oh, James. You're driving me crazy!" she cried.

"I plan to do more than that. I'm going to taste every inch of you." He sucked the other breast. He seated her on the edge of the bed and placed her heels upon the bedframe while pressing her knees back with his legs. She was totally exposed, and it excited her. Lizzy knew what was coming next. His kisses started to trail down to his goal. He kissed her inner thighs, causing more build-up of sensation in Lizzy.

"More!" she demanded.

So, he licked her clitoris until it was bright pink and swollen.

"Oh, God!" gasped Lizzy. She took her hands and ran them through his hair that she admired so much, then pressed his head into her. She wanted his whole face there. No shame. Just need. He started poking his tongue in and out, then exploring her depth. It was driving her mad with the need for more. He changed his strategy. He started to suck her womanhood. It made her spiral into a wild climax into his mouth. Yes, he had tasted all of her.

"Lizzy, you taste so good," James praised.

"Oh, James. I need to repay you." She knelt before him on the floor. With her right hand, she explored his shaft. She teased the tip, then replaced her fingers with her warm mouth. With her right hand, she pumped him, her tongue teasing his tip, then her whole mouth devouring him. Just when he was ready to explode, he lifted her head. Cum squirted over her hand and himself as he screamed his release. He opened the nightstand drawer and pulled out a reserved towel. After all was cleaned up, he threw the towel down to the ground.

"We're not done yet, Lizzy." He laid her across the bed with himself beside her. He kissed her as he inserted two fingers. He worked her until she was ready, and then he removed his fingers, positioned himself over her, and placed his shaft at her entrance. "Look into my eyes, Lizzy. I want to watch you come."

Slowly, he entered her, then did his dance, building up the pace until he was slamming into her. They saw and felt their love climax to heaven. Once he cleaned her, he gave her a kiss and said, "I love you with all my heart."

"I love you, too, James."

They cuddled and fell fast asleep.

—

The next day was early church and a quick lunch before James dressed in his uniform, kissed Lizzy goodbye, and was off to work. Lizzy had the rest of the afternoon to get everything ready for the girls. The girls arrived together at 6:00 PM. Alice picked everyone up. They liked the little touches Lizzy made around the house. They enjoyed dinner and opted to have dessert later.

Once all was cleared, Lizzy taught them to play hand-and-foot. Becky and Trish were partners. Alice was Lizzy's partner. Lizzy felt that playing cards with Alice bonded them. They talked about what Alice went through after Frank died. How the Musketeers and their wives helped her through it. Then, the conversation took a 360-degree turn. They wanted to know what it was like in bed with the sexy bachelor. Lizzy made several comments about being tired lately and a little sore walking. They all laughed. She even added that James gave a new meaning to having a spa bubble bath.

It was a little after 11:00 PM when Lizzy dished out the apple pie and ice cream. They decided to get together once a month, or whenever the guys had extra duty. They could even go to a movie and do dinner. Trish volunteered to host next month. They were laughing at a joke from Becky when the guys walked in.

"How was it?" asked Becky.

John walked up to her, bent down, and kissed her as he answered, "Good."

Carson and James did the same to their girls.

"What about me?" demanded Alice, so all three men went and kissed Alice on her cheek or forehead.

The ladies got up and cleared the table so the men could be served. John needed hot sauce. Everyone raved about the food. After pie was served, they wanted to know what time dinner was being served tomorrow.

It was a late night, and the guys needed their sleep for an early day. They hugged and said their goodbyes.

"How'd it go with the girls?" James asked.

"We had a great time. We're going to do this once a month and whenever you guys are on extra duty. Maybe take in a movie and dinner. They're a great group. I'm so glad they included me," Lizzy answered.

"I'm exhausted. I'm sure you are, too. Let's get some sleep."

They undressed and got under the covers.

"I love you, Lizzy."

"I love you, James."

They kissed, cuddled, and quickly fell asleep.

Chapter 13: The Special Date
November 18 and 19, 2021

Lizzy and James both attended several family dinners together. Marcy was pleasant and was slowly warming up to Lizzy. James still wanted to be with Lizzy when around his mom. Lizzy felt she was finally becoming part of the family.

They had her friends over for a barbecue. Jackie and her family came over for dinner and a game of Mexican Train. They took Alex and Leo to a UT football game, and they stayed overnight. It felt so right to everyone, especially Lizzy and James.

They attended an advancement ceremony with luncheon for a couple of other officers. Lizzy met the chief of police and more of James's coworkers. They had already built a life together in such a short time. James couldn't wait for Lizzy to get divorced so they could legally start their life. They talked about how it would take several months for it to be final. But to them, they already felt married.

James talked to his parents one day before getting home from work. He wanted to let them know he was proposing to Lizzy on Friday. He designed an engagement ring and would pick it up on Friday, so Lizzy didn't have time to find it. They said it was about time. Marcy admitted that Lizzy was perfect for him, and they were happy for both of them. Lizzy had much warmed up to Marcy as well.

James called Jackie and asked for her permission. He informed her about giving Lizzy a ring on Friday. She was excited and thought it was wonderful. She asked if she could do anything, but it was all up to him. He called Lizzy's sister Chris. They were all excited and planned on coming down Saturday to help celebrate. They would stay with Lizzy and James for a week-long visit. At the Thursday Musketeers' lunch, James told them his plan. They congratulated him and wished them the best of luck. He asked Carson to be his best man and John to be a groomsman. Carson agreed to go to lunch on Friday and stop at the jewelers to pick up the ring with James. They made jokes about James, the forever bachelor, finally falling in love.

Thursday night after making love, James told Lizzy he had a special evening planned for tomorrow, so there was no need for her to make dinner, just get dressed up. She hoped it was to ask her to marry him. They both couldn't wait for tomorrow evening.

Friday couldn't come fast enough for James. Reservations at Dancing Bear Restaurant were made along with an overnight stay in one of their best cabins. After a quick lunch, Carson drove them to the jewelers. They entered the store together. The owner quickly bent down to a drawer and pulled out a black velvet box.

"It's ready, Sheriff. Your design turned out gorgeous." He opened the box and placed it on the counter. The ring had a basket-type setting in the center for an oval diamond. Two ruby teardrops formed a heart shape on each side, all set in white gold.

"It's better than I envisioned," James complimented the man's workmanship. "She's going to love it."

"The matching wedding bands of intertwined circles will pair nicely with this," said the owner. He pulled out two more boxes and opened them. Engraved inside was, "Love you till the end of time."

James's heart raced, and he replied, "Thank you."

"It was a pleasure." The owner bagged the boxes.

James was glad that Carson drove because his mind was in the clouds. Once they were back at work, James placed the bags in his car's glove compartment. He hoped the rest of the day would pass by quickly. When 5:55 PM arrived, James organized his desk, said goodbye to all, and headed out to his car.

—

Hank cursed as he walked out of the prison. His hotheaded younger brother, Billy, was caught again late last night. A second offense for having possession of illegal substances with the intent to sell was the charge. He got into his decaying 1964, fading and chipped red C-10 Chevy pickup and slammed the door closed. He cursed again and lit a joint to help him think.

Why did those officers have to arrest Billy? Some of those officers grew up here. Didn't locals watch each other's backs and protect their own? Billy was just a tiny pea in a large kettle. Why don't they go after the big guys? Because they're rich and have political pull. Officers were all corrupt.

Hank pulled his two-gauge shotgun from under his seat, loaded it, cocked it, and placed it across his lap. He lit another joint. It was open season for the police, he decided. It was five to six, so he got out of his truck and slammed the door shut. The truck shielded him from the building but gave him a great view of the entrance and the parked vehicles. Gun in arm, Hank was ready.

A couple minutes later, the entrance to the station opened, and an officer stepped out. He walked behind another vehicle and stood there for a couple of seconds with his back to Hank. Here was the moment. Hank aimed at the officer's head, it was a nice head of hair, and fired. Perfect shot.

Who was next?

As Carson opened the door to exit, he saw it all happen in a blink of an eye. A man in torn-up jeans and a Vols T-shirt aiming his shotgun at James. Carson yelled as the shot was fired. At the same time, he unstrapped his holster, pulled out his gun, took the safety off, and aimed. The man turned toward Carson as James fell to the ground. The man started to aim at Carson, and Carson took a shot at the man's arm, but the man was still on target for Carson.

The man fired and just missed. Carson shot him in the chest. The man fell dead. Carson dropped his gun for other officers to pick up. He ran to James. The shot took the back of James's head right off. Carson fell to his knees and cried into his hands. His best friend, like a brother to him, had just died senselessly, years after Vietnam.

The chief knelt beside Carson.

"The shooter is dead. I'm so sorry, Carson. We all loved him like a brother. You had to kill the shooter, or you'd have been next."

Carson took a deep breath and wiped away the tears with his sleeve.

"What are we going to tell Lizzy? He was going to propose tonight," Carson said.

"First, go wash up. I'll talk to Chap. We'll go talk to his folks first, then Lizzy," Chief commanded.

"I'll call Alice and have her pack for a couple of days to stay with Lizzy," replied Carson.

"It's all we can do right now."

"First, I need to get the ring out of his car. I think she might want it right now." Carson opened the glove compartment and took out the bags, then placed them in his car and locked it.

As he approached the building, several officers were already outside collecting evidence and taking pictures as sirens were approaching. Carson walked into the restroom and started to shake. He ran to a stall, crouched down, and threw up. It was all so surreal. Once done, he walked shakily to the sink and braced himself. He looked into the mirror to see his shocked, ashen face. Quickly, he washed his hands and face with cold water. Once dry, he pulled out his phone and called Alice, then Trish to give her a heads-up that he would be late that night.

Once outside, he took a cold, deep breath, praying for God to give him courage and strength. The chief and chaplain were both waiting outside. They agreed to meet first at James's parents' house, then at Lizzy's. Marcy and Jimmy were in shock but always knew this could happen. The officers gave them all the details of time and events to come. All was set, so they didn't have to worry. After thirty minutes, they handed their cards in case Marcy or Jimmy needed anything or had questions. They then headed for Lizzy.

Alice pulled up to the house and left her keys in her purse beside her packed bag. She picked up the apple pie she had made that morning to use as an excuse to stop by. She hadn't cried yet. Shock will do that to you. Lizzy answered the doorbell.

"Hi! I made a pie and thought I'd drop it by for you. You look great in that blue dress. Am I interfering?" Alice greeted.

"Alice, thank you for the compliment and pie. Come in for a quick drink and talk before James gets home. He's taking me out for a special dinner."

"Sure. Diet ginger ale would be nice. Do you know where you're going?"

"No. It's a surprise," Lizzy giggled, then handed Alice her glass. Lizzy sat down on the couch with Alice. "The pie looks delicious. You're such a good cook." The doorbell rang. "Excuse me, Alice. It might be one of James's folks."

Lizzy's face turned ashen when she saw the chief, chaplain, and Carson with their caps in their hands, but no James. She started to pass out, but Chief caught her and helped her to the couch. She carefully laid down, and Alice covered her with a throw from the back of the couch.

"Oh, no," was all Lizzy could say, and she started to cry.

The chaplain started, "We are so sorry to tell you that James died instantly in a shooting."

He continued with times and events that would follow, then said a prayer.

Carson then spoke, "Alice will be with you twenty-four-seven until you feel okay. Trish and I will also help out, like we did with Alice. John and Becky will help with his parents."

While they talked to Lizzy, Alice brought her things into the guest bedroom. She then splashed whiskey into Lizzy's glass as the chaplain gave her more information about how to move forward. Carson placed a bag on the coffee table and took out a black velvet ring box.

"He planned a special dinner at the Dancing Bear, then an overnight stay at their best cabin. I don't know when he planned his proposal, but it was tonight. He designed this special ring just for you." Carson handed her the ring and placed the box on the table. She placed it on her ring finger, and her eyes teared up, but she wanted to keep control until they left. She knew how hard it was on these men to do this.

"It's beautiful," she whispered.

"Oh, Lizzy. It is beautiful," exclaimed Alice.

"There are matching wedding bands in the bag," Carson said sadly.

"The rings should go to Vickie and Jeff. It can be our wedding gift to them. I think James would like that," Lizzy replied.

"I'll drop them off tomorrow," Carson assured her. "Get some rest. We are so sorry for your loss. Here are our cards if you need us for anything or have any questions." He placed their cards on the table. "Try and get some sleep. I'll be back tomorrow afternoon." He kissed her forehead. "Thanks for coming, Alice."

He kissed her forehead, too. The men left, and Alice locked the door. Alice sat and cuddled Lizzy while she cried until she couldn't anymore. Alice handed Lizzy her ginger ale with the added whiskey and said, "Drink this down. It will help you sleep." Lizzy quickly drank the ginger ale mix. "Now, take a shower, put on a nightgown, and get some sleep."

They walked into her bedroom, and Alice let her take her time to get ready. Alice tucked her into bed and asked, "Is there anything you want or anything I can do for you?"

"Call my sister, Vickie, and Michael. I need someone to pick up my sister and brother-in-law tomorrow from the airport."

"I'll take care of it before I go to bed. This month is going to go fast and be unbelievable, but you will get through it. I'm here twenty-four-seven for you until you're okay, Lizzy," Alice said.

"Thanks, Alice. I really appreciate it."

Alice turned the lights off. "I'm leaving the door open in case you need me. Just yell, and I'll be right here."

Alice went to the guest bathroom and showered, dressed in her nightgown, and got into bed. She made the calls needed. Michael was nice enough to pick up Chris and her husband. Everyone was shocked. Alice quickly said a prayer and went to sleep.

Chapter 14: The Promise
November 20, 2021

"Lizzy, wake up. Lizzy, wake up," whispered a soft, familiar male voice. Lizzy groggily opened her eyes. To her surprise, she found James standing beside the bed, looking down at her.

"James, is that you? I thought you were dead," she asked, confused. Slowly, she sat up.

"Yes, Lizzy," he replied, "I am dead. I've come for you so that we can start anew."

He covered her hands and helped her out of bed.

"I can't live without you, James. It's unbearable. It hurts too much."

"I know, Lizzy." He embraced her lovingly. "I hope next time, we start young, so we have a lot more time. This was way too short." He looked into her eyes. "Lizzy, I will always love you. In every lifetime, until the end of time."

"James, I will always love you," replied Lizzy. "In every lifetime."

They kissed and then faded away.

Until next time.

About the Author

Cindy M. Rankin was born and grew up in Illinois. She is a graduate of Northeastern Illinois University. She married Wayne in 1974.

They have a son, daughter, son-in-law, and two grandsons. They have lived in Illinois, Texas, Michigan, and Virginia, and now reside in Tennessee.

Cindy loves gardening, crocheting, cooking, baking, painting, games, movies, and books.

This is her first book. She had a recurring dream for twenty years, which is Part II of this story. Recently at a luncheon with lady friends, a sheriff came to their table and stared at her like he was trying to signal an interest but was just kidding around. This gave her the spark to write this trilogy. Part III was written, but Cindy needed the story to start somewhere. With research came Part I. Her friend Joan advised her to include tarot cards, which developed into the high priestess, a gypsy palm reader, and a tarot card reader.

She hopes you enjoy the book and think about when, what, and who comes next!

Help authors like Cindy M. Rankin reach more readers by posting reviews online.

If you enjoyed and want to comment on this book, please write to Crippled Beagle Publishing. If you have a book idea or manuscript and are interested in publishing your story, contact Crippled Beagle Publishing.

Visit www.crippledbeaglepublishing.com.

www.ingramcontent.com/pod-product-compliance
Lightning Source LLC
Chambersburg PA
CBHW071603180626
46819CB00002B/112